P.S. Longer Letter Later

P.S. Longer Letter Later

PAULA DANZIGER
& ANN M. MARTIN

Scholastic Press New York

Ann and Paula would like to acknowledge Laura Godwin for coming up with the concept for this book, Elisa Geliebter for typing the manuscript, and Bruce Coville for his valuable suggestions.

Library of Congress Cataloging-in-Publication Data

Danziger, Paula
P.S. longer letter later/by Paula Danziger and Ann M. Martin.
p. cm.
Summary: Twelve-year-old best friends Elizabeth and Tara-Starr continue their friendship through letter-writing after Tara-Starr's family moves to another state.
ISBN 0-590-21310-5
[1. Friendship—Fiction. 2. Moving, Houshold—Fiction.
3. Letters—Fiction.] I. Martin, Ann M. II. Title.
PZ7.D2394Lo 1998
[Fic]—dc21   97-19120
                                                              CIP
                                                              AC

Printed in the U.S.A.
First edition, April 1998
Book design by Jessica Shatan

For Kathy Ames,
who knows how to introduce friends.

—P.D. & A.M.M.

Elizabeth

September 4

Dear Tara-Starr,

It's 4:02 P.M. and I'm sitting in my room at the end of the first day of seventh grade, and I can't help what I'm going to say next.

I AM SO MAD AT YOU. WHY DID YOU HAVE TO MOVE AWAY??? I *THOUGHT* WE WERE SUPPOSED TO BE BEST FRIENDS 4-EVER. IF I DIDN'T LIKE YOU SO MUCH I WOULD HAVE MADE YOU MY EX-BEST FRIEND 4-EVER BY NOW.

Okay. There. I just had to say that. I'm not *really*

mad. You're still my best friend. I hate that you moved away, but I know it wasn't your fault.

So . . . you want to know the highlights of the day? I get off the bus, I walk into Reston Middle School, and right away I notice that

1. Mr. Chimanto (however you spell his name) grew a mustache and it looks nice.

2. Mme. Simon got her hair all cut off and she looks like a boiled owl.

3. Joelie* *may* have gotten a nose job. No one can tell. (Here I sense that you would make some sort of nose/knows pun, but I'm not good at puns like you are so you can fill in your own.) _____

_____

Another highlight involves Karen Frank, Barf Queen of the Water Fountain. Remember how she has barfed in the water fountain on the first day of school every year? Well, she didn't let us down today.

*Joelie Hammond, in case you don't remember.

In fact, she let it all up. Again. And to make things even more interesting, she barfed right in front of about 15 girls who were all discussing Joelie's nose, and she *almost* started a chain reaction.

You know what I don't understand? How can the *Wheel of Fortune* home game have 400 puzzles but over 11 *million* categories? This does not make sense, but it's what I heard the announcer say when I was channel surfing last night. (Emma and I are still not allowed to be Wheel Watchers. This won't change as long as Dad only lets us watch educational shows. The only place I ever got to see *WOF* was at your house. Now what am I supposed to do?)

Well, that's it for now. Write and tell me about your first day of school. I know you don't start until tomorrow. I guess that's one of the benefits of moving to Ohio. As far as I can tell, though, it's the *only* benefit.

Love,
Elizabeth

P.S. Emma started at Miss Fine's Preschool today and she hated it. She says she already learned everything on *Sesame Street,* plus, she doesn't like crackers.

September 7

Dear Elizabeth,

GIVE ME A BREAK!!!!!!!!!!!!!

YOU KNOW THAT I DIDN'T WANT TO MOVE . . . THAT I WAS KIDNAPPED BY THE CHARENTS (my CHildlike pARENTS). . . . Oh, okay . . . I know that it's not kidnapping if your parents want to move and their kid has to go with them. . . . I know I should be used to it by this time. . . . Fourth, fifth, sixth grades. . . . It was a record for staying in one place.

Anyway, it was sooooooooooooooo weird not starting school with you.

The night before school began here, I was soooooooo homesick. . . . Not just for my old home . . . but for yours too. I kept thinking about how the nights before fifth and sixth grade we would go to each other's houses and figure out what each of us would wear for the first day of school. I was soooooo sad. I took out my copy of the scrapbooks we made before I left and looked at the pictures Barb took of us on our first days of school. . . .

Fourth grade — you wearing that plaid skirt and the white blouse, loafers, and your mom's pearl earrings. I had on my black leggings with a hole in one knee, my long black T-shirt with SAVE THE WHALES on it, my black high-tops with the pink fluorescent laces, and my mom's black-and-pink beaded barrette.

Fifth grade — your *new* look!!!! Plaid skirt, white blouse, loafers, and your mom's gold-and-pearl earrings. *My* new look!!!! The same leggings, more black high-tops with the same fluorescent laces, a black T-shirt that says SAVE THE HUMANS, and my mom's clip-on nose ring.

Sixth grade — you wore that "cute" flowered sundress, preppy sandals, and your mom's pearl nose ring (just kidding). I wore new black leggings (holeless), black sandals, a black T-shirt that said

IF YOU CAN READ THIS,

YOU'RE TOO CLOSE

and my dad's hoop earring.

Thanks for filling me in on the gossip. As for the pun about Joelie's possible face surgery, how about "Nobody nose for sure if she had it done. . . . It's snot something she's talking about." Okay . . . it's not one of my best puns, but since I've moved, I haven't had anyone to tell them to.

I need more first-day details. . . . So what did you wear? I want to know. I wore my black leggings, my long black T-shirt (sloganless), my red Doc Martens, and around my head I wore one of Barb's glitter scarves. (You know . . . the one she had on at "Back to School Night," when all of the teachers thought she was my older sister . . . not my mother.)

Anyway . . . my first day of school went okay . . . as well as it could with me being the new kid in the school, not knowing anyone, not knowing my way around.

A few of the kids made fun of the way I was dressed. One of the boys, Alex, asked me if I was a fortune-teller. I told him that I could see a major disaster in his future if he continued teasing me.

School lunch was not only disgusting, but I had no one to sit with.

My classes are okay . . . except for the fact that there don't seem to be any writing classes. How am I going to become a great American writer (with our novels next to each other on bookshelves) if there's no time for creative writing?

By the way, I've made a slight change in my name. At first, I thought about starting out anew with a name like Mary or Sarah or Jane. Then I would change my look and my goals . . . but that didn't seem right, so instead of Tara-Starr Lane . . . my new name is Tara*Starr Lane. . . . Isn't that much more exciting looking?

I have to go now. Barb and Luke are going to be home from work in about a half an hour and I've got to set the table. (What wonderful meal has Jeannemarie prepared for your family tonight? Her herbed chicken? Her caramelized carrots? Her chocolate parfait? *Our* dinner will be hamburgers, french fries, and beverages supplied by McDonald's and delivered by Luke, and cake prepared by Sara Lee.)

Love,

Tara Starr

P.S. I'm so proud of Emma for hating Miss Fine's Preschool. I'll never understand why your parents have to send their kids to a private preschool whose motto is THE PLACE FOR A FINE EDUCATION.

I've really got to go now. The Charents will be home any minute.

Elizabeth

September 11
5:36 P.M.

Dear Tara*Starr,

Ha-ha. Very funny. You know perfectly well that Miss Fine's does not have a pun for a motto. They don't have enough imagination for that. Their motto is . . . well, actually, they don't have one.

Hmm. I just reread your letter for, like, the tenth time. I keep reading it over and over because it's SORT OF like having you here with me. I keep looking at my copy of our scrapbooks too. Remember the day we made them? Mom couldn't believe we were making such a mess right after Martha had cleaned up. (If I just keep that footstool three inches off center, it covers the toeprint you accidentally made that day. Don't you think there's something funny about a *foot*stool covering a *toe*print?)

I miss you so much! And it's all the Charents' fault. Charents. I like that word. It's ugly, which is a good thing, since I'm mad at the Charents. Later, if I get over being mad at them, maybe I'll decide it's a nice word. Anyway, I keep reading the letter, but what I really want is to talk to you and I can't believe we can't even call each other. You at least have a good excuse, since the Charents say it's too expensive. I can understand that. But my dad is just being strict as usual. "No phoning Tara." (How come he'll never call you Tara*Starr?)

Oh, well. Now I've read your letter for the 11th time and I'm going to answer all your questions in the order you asked them.

1. On the first day of school, I wore jeans, loafers, and a white blouse. Plus, Mom helped me French-braid my hair and lent me her gold hoop earrings.

2. I don't know how you're going to become a great American writer if there's no time for creative writing — except you can make your own time for it. Why don't you try keeping a notebook (and not losing it)? This year I have Mr. Dougherty for creative writing, so things are off to a good start. (I do wish you had a writing class, though. I'd be disappointed too if I didn't have one.)

3. Yes, Tara*Starr is much more exciting than Tara-Starr. I love it. What can you do for Elizabeth? Maybe I need a change too.

4. For dinner after the first day of school Jeannemarie made pork chops, string beans, and a salad. And she made crème brûlée for dessert. Dad missed dinner entirely because of some emergency meeting at Data-Pro. Sometimes being a vice president isn't worth it. I don't know about Dad, but I'd take pork chops over a meeting any day.

Emma just came into the room. Now she's standing at my elbow, asking me what I'm doing. I tell her

I'm writing you a letter and she says she misses you. She does, too. She thinks you're funny. I'm going to try to be funnier for her.

Love,

Elizabeth ☺

P.S. I'm really proud of you for being the new kid at school and being so brave about it and telling that kid you saw a disaster in his future. I would *never* be able to be so brave. Have you made any friends yet?

P.P.S. I don't think Emma hates Miss Fine's so much anymore. They have Day-Glo Play-Doh.

Sept. 16

Dear Tara*Starr,

Guess what. Grandpa called and said come down to Vero Beach for the weekend. (Nana was going to be away for the weekend and he didn't want to be alone.) So we all went to Florida for three days, but it wasn't really a vacation. Emma caught a fish. But she was *very* sad that she did not get to see Mickey Mouse.

Love,

Elizabeth ☺

P.S. How come you never answered my last letter? Are you mad at me?

September 21

Dear Elizabeth

No . . . I AM NOT ANGRY AT YOU. . . . At least I wasn't until I got the postcard telling me that you jetted off to Florida. . . . What a rough life!!!!!!

Well, maybe I am just a little angry. . . . Well, maybe I am a lot angry . . . but don't take it personally. I think I'm just angry at everything in the world at the moment.

I'm sorry that I haven't written for two weeks. I was going to send you a dumb cute note saying that I hadn't written because I lost my pen . . . but that's not true. . . . I think I haven't written because I've lost my sanity . . . and my sense of humor . . . and my temper.

It's all just so hard sometimes. . . . My parents are acting weird. (Actually, they are acting normal . . . which is so weird!) Both of them have jobs that they like. . . . And my mother is going to a parenting class . . . a parenting class . . . do you believe it? I'm twelve years old, she's twenty-nine, and NOW she's going to a parenting class. . . . Maybe she should have gone when I was born . . . but NOW??????? She just says that she wants to be the best mother to me that she can be . . . that she wants to make up for all the years that she wasn't as grown up as she should have been. And my dad is making "dad noises," like, "Now that we are saving to buy a house, we all have to economize." Can you believe that this is coming from my Charents? . . . I'm so used to being the one who is responsible that this is really weird . . . and a real pain. Do you believe . . . they are actually giving me a curfew . . . and what's even more disgusting than the curfew is that I have no place to go, no place to come back late from. (Wow . . . that sentence is definitely a run-on, fragmenty, ended-with-a-preposition sentence. . . . I know all of this now because Ms. Fishburn, my language arts teacher, . . . yes, that's her name, but secretly I think of her as Ms. Tunamelt . . . loves grammar and sentence structure.) Oh, well, back to the Charent Report.

First, they make me move to a new place (which isn't so unusual for them) and then they start acting so different.

I can tell you . . . I DON'T LIKE IT!!!!!

And . . . you know what else I don't like . . . I don't like my new school. Everyone's so stuck-up and mean . . . and they make fun of the way I dress . . . and Ms. Tunamelt doesn't like my writing. . . . She says, "It's too creative. It's not academic enough." And she looks gross too. . . . She wears the same outfit every day in different colors . . . a skirt, a blouse, and a jacket. Monday, she wears her pale blue combo . . . Tuesday is puke green . . . Wednesday is you-know-what brown . . . Thursday is warning-light yellow . . . and Friday is pot-holder plaid.

I kept waiting to write back until I was happy, but if I did that you probably wouldn't hear from me until graduation day.

Okay . . . enough. . . . To change the subject.

I can't believe that you and your family just jetted off to Florida. I am so jealous. Did Emma wear the sunglasses that I gave her, the ones your parents hate . . . the ones with palm trees and glitter on them? The ones your father says are so tacky?

Now . . . to talk about the stuff in your letter . . .

1. I keep looking at the scrapbooks too. You know what really makes me laugh? Remember the summer I went on vacation with your family, and then you went on vacation with my family? I love the picture of you and my family at the county fair — we look great with cotton candy all over our faces. Even the lime-green poodle we won has cotton candy on his face. Then there's the picture of me with your family at the art museum in the city. It was sooooo nice to be included in one of your many family trips, even though I know your father really hates me.

2. About the creative writing . . . At the moment, the only creative writing is my letters to you . . . but maybe that's more nonfiction. I think I have writer's block.

3. Possible Elizabeth name change . . . Liz, Lizzy, Lizzylu, Beth, Bethie, Betherino, Elizarino, Eliza, Liza, Zabeth (I really like that one), El, Clyde, Waldo, Richie (for Richardson, not for the amount of money you have). Tell Emma I love her and miss her soooooooooooooo much.

Bye.

Tara Starr

P.S. (As in Positively Sorry) Oh, Elizabeth . . . I just reread this letter . . . and I apologize for being so mean at the beginning of it. I guess I'm just upset . . . and yes, angry . . . at everything . . . and I'm taking it out on you.

Now you know why I haven't written for so long.

September 25
4:35 P.M.

Dear Tara-Starr,

Okay, so I was right. You *are* mad at me. And you're right too. You *were* very mean in your so-called letter. Where do you get off taking it out on me? I know what that makes me, because we just learned about it in social studies. It makes me the scapegoat, which is not an attractive thing — for me (the scapegoat) or for you (the scapegoat-maker). If you're feeling so very friendless right now, then I suggest

20

treating me a little differently. That is, if you think I'm still your friend.

I'm tempted to end this letter right here and mail just these two paragraphs to you, but I know that's too rude. Instead, I'm going to go back through your letter from the beginning. I have a few things to ask you about anyway. And a few more things to say.

For starters, I wouldn't exactly call flying to Orlando on a Friday morning with 4,000 people who are all going to Disney World "jetting off to Florida." You make it sound like we went on a private jet. (Well . . . we did fly first class, but you know my dad. And it's no fun being in first class. We're almost always the only kids, and everyone acts like they wish we weren't there.) And then we had to get in a stuffy rental car and drive to Vero Beach, whizzing right past all the signs for Disney World, which are the only 2 words Emma knows how to read.

Plus, we got tricked into going down there in the first place, which you would know *if* you read my postcard carefully.

So your parents are acting normal. Can't you be a little grateful? Two happy parents, saving for their own *house*. Maybe it means you won't have to move again. Sometimes you don't know how lucky you are. Barb *wants* to work and she *gets* to work. My mom wants to work and my dad says he makes enough money so she doesn't need a job. She's to stay home and manage the house and the people who work in it. I know my dad only wants what he thinks is best for our family, but doesn't he see how bored Mom is? At *your* house, nobody's ever bored.

No, Emma did not wear the sunglasses you gave her. She lost them over the summer.

All right. I think I've said enough.

Elizabeth

Oh, Tara. I just reread this letter because I always reread letters before I mail them in case I find a spelling mistake or maybe a punctuation error. And it was a good thing, because I found an ENORMOUS mistake. And not the kind of mistake like "there" for "their" or no question mark, but, like, a mistake in my thinking.

All of a sudden, I understand something else about scapegoats, something Mr. Chiumento (now I know how to spell his name) forgot to tell us. He forgot to tell us how easy it is to make someone a scapegoat. And he forgot to tell us how if you get angry enough you don't even think about who you're taking your anger out on. See, when I got your letter today I thought, Great, now I can tell Tara about what's been happening around here, which is not good. (I mean, what's happening is not good.) Then I opened your letter and read it, and I got mad about the things you had said. And I took it out on you — even though I really do still consider you my best, *best,* BEST friend in the whole world ever. So I apologize for everything I said — but I'm still mailing this letter because I do sort of mean the things, just in a nicer way.

I'm really sorry you have writer's block. That's bad, but I don't think it will last.

The thing I wanted to tell you about concerns my dad. He hasn't been home before 11:00 P.M. for a week. And Mom won't talk about it. She gets that leave-me-alone-I-can't-talk-about-it look. I really have so much to tell you, but now I'm just plain too tired. This is not an attention-getter. Like, now I want you to write back and *beg* me to tell you what's wrong. I really am too tired after writing the mad part of this letter. I PROMISE I'll tell you the other stuff in my next letter.

Your friend 4-ever,

Elizabeth ☺

P.S. Tara, can't you come up with a better nickname for me? I know you weren't trying before because you were mad. And this is really important.

P.P.S. The next time I write I'll put the * back in your name.

Dear Eliza*Beth (That's your new nickname. Do you like it? I really REALLY do. . . . It's kind of like you . . . a little old-fashioned but willing to try new things. And if you add the star, then we can be the Star-twins or the Star-friends or just the Stars. . . . And you don't have to change the spelling of your name or anything. . . . So let me know what you think of it.)

I could go on for pages about why I'm sorry that I said all of that stuff . . . but you already know that I'm sorry.

To answer your questions:

1. About mentioning that your father doesn't like me — I know you don't like to think about that, but it's true. But just because my parents got married so young and we've never had much money is no reason for him to act like that. After all, your parents weren't always so rich, were they? (Actually, I know that you didn't question me about your dad. . . . I just wanted to say this.)

2. I'm sorry that you are so upset that your father hasn't been home at night until late. Do you think it's work? Do you think it's something else . . . or someone else?

About what's happening with me — nothing much. . . . It's still the same.

Write back soon.

Your Star-Friend (*Friend for short),

Tara Starr

October 2

Dear Tara*Starr,

I love my new name! And I love being the Stars or Star-Twins or Star-Friends or *Friends, but mostly I just like being friends, which I'm glad we still are. I'm glad we're over our letter-fight. (If our parents would just let us *talk,* we probably could have cleared things up even more quickly.)

Well, I PROMISED I would tell you about my dad, so here goes. Remember when I said he hasn't been home before 11:00 for a week? Well, that was a whole week ago, and he *still* hasn't come home before

11:00, so now that makes two weeks. And one night I don't know *what* time he came home because it was so long after 11:00 that I guess I was sound asleep.

I know, I know. You're thinking that he probably didn't come home until the morning, but I'm sure he did. When he left for work, Mom asked him if he would try to get home before four. And somehow I just knew she meant get home before four in the morning, not four in the afternoon, like she sometimes used to ask him to do if we were going out to dinner together or something. What could my dad possibly be doing every night until 11:00 or 4:00?

You asked if it was some*thing* or some*one*. (Only you would ask me that.) And I thought about it, and I really think it's some*thing*. Don't ask me why. I just have a feeling.

Guess what. Mom asked me to play with Emma today while she went downtown. I said okay because of course I have no friends and no life since you've gone, so I have nothing to do but homework. (Oh, and I started a new cross-stitch project.) Anyway, Emma asked for some apple juice, so I went to the pantry, and guess what I found behind all the juice and seltzer and stuff. Four big bottles of vodka. I mean those *really* big bottles, like gallons or something. That's a lot, isn't it? Maybe Mom and Dad are going to have a party, but they usually tell me so ahead of time. If those bottles *aren't* for a party, well, I don't know. My stomach felt all cold and watery when I saw them.

So, Tara, tell me about some of the kids in your school. Are there *any* potential friends? Do you ever see the boy whose future you predicted on the first day of school? Are there any normal kids? Are there any other new kids you could hook up with? Like, maybe you could join together and form a group of your own . . . all the new kids. Hey, maybe Ms. Heartburn or whatever has a daughter at the school. You could become her new best friend and get on Ms. Heartburn's good side.

Well, here's Emma. I think she wants to add something to the letter. I better give her a new page.

EMMA

That's all for now.

Your Best *Friend Forever,

Eliza * Beth ☺

October 10

Dear Eliza*Beth,

I'm so glad that you love your new name. Are you going to start using it at school, putting it on all of your homework, having everyone call you by that name? You really should.

I want to talk about the stuff in your letter. I'm a little worried . . . actually I'm a LOT worried!!!!!!!!!!!!!!! It definitely does not sound good at your house.

What is happening to your father? Are things bad at work? Are he and your mother fighting?

(I know your parents always act like everything is perfect . . . but what's going on seems REALLY weird.)

I talked to Barb about some of the stuff in your letter. (Okay. You know that I never lie to you. . . . I showed my mom your letter. I didn't think you would mind. . . . You always used to talk to her when you came over to the house . . . and you know she really cares about you. . . . So I hope you don't mind that I let her see what you wrote.) Barb said that any time you really need her, you can call and reverse the charges. (She knows how your parents don't like you to call me.) When she said that about the call, I begged to call you but she said no . . . this offer was for emergencies only. (We are on a really tight budget . . . as usual!!!!!!!)

Why aren't you hanging out with any of the kids there? I know you used to ride with some of them at the stables, before I moved to town.

And even though they aren't really your *friends*, you could do things with them or with some of the other kids. (You really shouldn't be so shy. . . . You are so nice and so funny once someone gets to know you.) But Eliza*Beth, a lot of kids do like you. You just have to call them, invite them over to your house, hang out with them more. I know they're probably not the kids your father would want as your friends, but they're the ones *you* want as your friends. (I just got a letter from Sarah, and she was talking about trying out for the school play. Why don't you get involved with the Drama Club? You are sooooo good in art. . . . Maybe you could cross-stitch the scenery . . . just kidding. . . . Really, you could do scenery or costumes . . . or maybe even try out for the play. That would a good way to be with people, to have fun.)

Actually, I've decided to take my own advice. I'm going to try out for the Drama Club play . . . and the school newspaper . . . and for Future Corpses of America. (People are just dying to get into that club. . . . I know . . . I know . . . it's a dumb old joke, but it's been a hard time for me and I'm just getting back my sense of humor.) Really, though, I am going to get involved with drama and writing. I'm getting soooooooo bored with being bored.

You asked me about the kids at my school.

First of all, there are soooooooooo many more of them. This school is gigantic. It's one of those regional ones that kids from a lot of towns go to.

(I never thought about how lucky we were to live in a small town with its own schools. Here kids go to schools in their own towns until sixth grade. Then they go to a school for seventh through ninth grade. High school is tenth through twelfth grades. Whew!!!!!!!!!!!!!!!!

The good news for me is that this is a new school for ALL seventh-graders. (Well . . . it's new for all seventh-graders except for the ones who flunked last year. . . . One of them is in my gym class. His name is Hank. I think of him as Hank the Tank.)

The bad news is that everyone else seems to have come from one of the small-town schools . . . and they all know other people. I haven't found anyone else who moved here from somewhere else.

There seem to be certain groups at this school.

1. The really popular "we are so perfect" group. They make me want to barf. They seem to make the "rules" about how to be, what to wear.

2. The "we live in the detention room after school" group.

3. The "we love being different" group. There are all kinds of kids in this group. Actually, there are a few I want to get to know.

4. The social misfits. . . . There are a lot of kids in this group who I am going to try to get to know.

5. The "A list" . . . the kids who really care about their grades and spend a lot of time studying.

6. The everyone else group . . . in case I left anyone out. You know how I hate to see anyone left out.

Elizabeth . . . I've just looked at what I've written. I sound like such a snot. (I know that you hate that word.) I really do sound like one, though. You know how I hate when people label other people. . . . AND I'VE JUST DONE THAT!!!! How gross! I've got to get out of this rotten mood.

Oh, well. . . . I'm not going to let it get to me. I'm going to do something to work all of this out. You know me. I'm not the kind of person who looks at a half-filled glass and sees it as half empty . . . or half full either. I always figure that I can do some-thing to fill it to the top.

I've got to go now. I'm going to try out for the play.

I want the lead . . . I want to be the star.
LOVE,

Tara Starr

Elizabeth

Dear Tara*Starr,

That was so cool of your mom to say I can call her and reverse the charges. I'll probably do it sometime, even though I don't know *how* to reverse the charges. I guess I just call the operator and tell her what I want to do???

Anyway, I really miss your mom. And your dad. (Since I'm not mad at them anymore, I've decided "Charents" is a nice word after all.) Mostly I miss you, though. Tara, don't you think you could convince the Charents to come back here for a little visit? You could all drive out here one weekend. We wouldn't have to figure out anything complicated, like how to get you here by yourself. Then I could see Barb and Luke too. Please? PLEASE? Just ask them about it, okay? If you can't afford a motel, maybe you could stay at Sarah's or something.

I liked hearing about the kids at your school. Have you tried to get to know anyone in the "we love being different group" yet? Or any of the social misfits? If I went to your school, I guess I'd be one of the social misfits. I wonder if I'd like it. I suppose if there were enough of us I wouldn't think much about it. Besides, I'd rather belong to the social misfit group than to no group at all.

So did you try out for the play? YOU HAVE TO TELL ME WHAT HAPPENED. I'm dying to know!!! Did you get a part? A big part? Are you the star? I wish we lived closer. Then I'd come see you in the play. No matter what part you get I'll be *so* proud of you. (I know you'll get *some* part.)

I haven't talked to anyone about the Drama Club yet. I don't really have time for an activity. I have to baby-sit for Emma most afternoons. Mom is busy almost *all* the time working on PTA stuff and now also for this group called Kate's Kitchen that helps feed hungry families here. (Mom told me the way it works, which is really neat, but it takes a long time to explain, so I'll save it for another letter.) Anyway, I wrote this while Emma was napping, and now she's calling to me from her room.

Gotta go.

Love,

Eliza Beth

(I love my name!!!)

P.S. PLEASE PLEASE PLEASE think about visiting.

October 25

Dear Eliza*Beth . . . .

Earth to Eliza*Beth!!!!!!!!!!!!!!!!!!!!!!!!!!!!!!!!!!!! I can't believe that you didn't discuss the stuff going on with your family. Please. . . . Enquiring minds want to know.

As for coming to visit you. I WOULD LOVE TO . . . AND SO WOULD THE CHARENTS!!! But you know we really don't have the bucks to do that. For the first time in ages, both of my parents are making good money. (Good for our family — maybe not as good as a lot of families, but for us . . . good.) That means the bills are being paid and a very little bit of money is being saved. Trips are out of the question right now. Also, Sarah's house isn't big enough. (Might I remind you that your house is gigantic? But I know your parents would have heart attacks if my family showed up at your house. I know . . . you would have us stay there if it was your choice.)

Now for my news. I TRIED OUT FOR THE PLAY AND I GOT A PART . . . NOT JUST ANY PART BUT ONE OF THE LEADS. . . . I'M GOING TO PLAY DOROTHY IN *THE GIZZARD OF OZ.* (It's the heart-warming story about a girl from Kansas who gets caught in a tornado, ends up in Australia, and has to get help from a chicken part.)

Okay . . . I'm joking.

The play that they're doing is *Cheaper by the Dozen,* which was chosen so that lots of kids could have parts. I'm Anne, one of twelve kids in a family that is run by efficiency experts (not exactly like my family, which has been run by no one — since my parents are sometimes inefficiency experts). AND GUESS WHAT . . . Alex, the kid who teased me in the beginning, plays one of my brothers, and it turns out he's also my neighbor. PLUS . . . Hank the Tank plays my father. Oh, well. I'm used to having a young father.

As for making new friends, I'm doing better.

Kids are talking to me a lot more.

You know how I did it? I decided to say at least one sentence to at least fifteen people a day and I smile at them when I say it.

Here are some of my sentences:

"Hi, how are you?" "Please pass the catsup?" (I ask this no matter what I'm eating . . . yesterday it was an ice cream sandwich.) "Your fly is unzipped." "Is that spinach on your tooth?" "Have you noticed that a snot ball has escaped from your nose?"

Needless to say, I am becoming one of the most popular kids in the school.

Just kidding again.

I don't use those sentences.

I am, however, trying out less obnoxious sentences and IT'S WORKING!!!!!!!!!!!! I really have met some new kids . . . more about that later. . . . Right now, I've got to go downstairs. Barb is going to help me figure out a costume. . . . At school we're going to have a combination Halloween costume and come as your favorite book character party. (It's a little "baby" but it'll be fun and I'm thinking of going as either the Cat in the Hat, the Little Engine That Could, or Elizabeth Bennett—*Pride and Prejudice* is my new favorite book). Gotta rush . . . see you.

Love,

Tara Starr

P.S. I was trying not to mention this because I know it will upset you . . . but what is this about your not having time for an activity at school because you have to baby-sit for Emma? Is this a bogus excuse? What happened to Jeannemarie and Martha? Why don't your parents hire a nanny? Also, why is Emma still taking naps? Does she feel well? Is she bored? Upset? Out late on dates?

October 31

Dear Tara*Starr,

Well, here it is Halloween and I'm not going out or anything. I guess you're probably at the combination costume and book character party right now. What costume did you decide on? Personally, I'm voting for the Cat in the Hat or the Little Engine That Could. No offense, but Elizabeth Bennett doesn't sound all that interesting, although I haven't read *Pride and Prejudice* yet. (By the way, I just started *The Yearling* and I can barely put it down.) There's no party at school this year. Nancy Hall (remember her?

44

from down the street?) invited me to go trick-or-treating with her and her sister and their cousin, but I feel too old for trick-or-treating. I took Emma trick-or-treating this afternoon, though. We went at 3:30 because Emma just couldn't wait any longer. Emma's costume was one of those horrible plastic ones from March's downtown. She's supposed to be a skeleton, but it's hard to tell. I guess you get what you pay for, and Mom paid about three dollars for this thing — when she finally even remembered that Emma would need a costume, which was at, like, 9:00 last night.

A little different from last year, huh? Remember the good old days when my family was normal? (Well, normal for *my* family.) Tara, you're right. Something BIG is going on. And believe me, I'm waking up and smelling the coffee. I just don't like what I smell. I tried to get away with holding my nose, but even I know that doesn't make the odor go away. That's like trying to fix a leaky faucet by closing the door to the bathroom so you can't hear the dripping anymore.

But anyway, *do* you remember last year? Last year Mom asked Emma and me in September what we wanted to be for Halloween, and by the middle of October those elaborate handmade costumes were finished. Last year Mom used to stay at home all day being a mom. Last year Dad used to come home at six most nights and then we would eat dinner together. I know you think he's a stuffed shirt, but he was always planning things for Emma and me. And most important, he was home every evening and every weekend.

So back to Halloween. It's *so* different this year. It didn't even occur to Mom to buy Emma a pumpkin. In fact, she forgot to buy Halloween candy too. She's downstairs now handing out gum, breath mints, apples, even those mini boxes of cereal — anything she can find. It's *so* embarrassing.

So. What *is* going on in my house? Well, here's the thing. I'm not sure.

But I have my suspicions.

I know you think Dad is having an affair (you *do* watch a lot of television), but like I said before, I'm pretty sure that's not it. I still couldn't tell you why. It's just a very strong feeling. And you know that when I get my *really* strong feelings I'm usually right.

What I think is going on (but I do NOT have a *strong* feeling about) is that Mom and Dad are getting a divorce. I just can't figure out *why.* I haven't heard one single word about what's wrong between them. Usually when parents are getting divorced the kids have *some* idea about it. Like all Carly heard about for months before her parents got divorced was how they fought over money. I mean, a neon divorce sign was practically beaming from their rooftop.

My only clues are that my family is so different from last year, and that my parents seem really unhappy and all wrapped up in themselves. I guess that spells DIVORCE.

But I'm not sure.

To answer your questions — baby-sitting for Emma is not a bogus excuse. As you well know, Martha leaves at 3:00, and Jeannemarie was hired to *cook.* Plus, Emma and I don't *want* a nanny. I suppose I could ask Mom to get a sitter for her, but the thing is that Mom races off nearly every afternoon now and I feel kind of sorry for Emma. She looks confused. Besides, she's my little sister and I love her. I'd rather watch her myself than let someone else do it. Anyway, what's the point of getting a sitter when *I* don't have anywhere to go? Mom would probably hire, like, Carly — to be *my* sitter? Forget it.

And Tara, Emma takes naps because she's *four*. Most kids nap until they're five or six, which you would know if you had a little sister. I think preschool takes a lot out of Emma. On school days she absolutely crashes at about three-thirty in the afternoon. On weekends she sometimes doesn't nap, though. But by six o'clock on those days we all wish she did.

Well, this has been an extremely long letter about me. But guess what. Now that it's written, I feel better. I wish we could talk in person, though. I love Barb, but I want to talk to *you*.

Love,

Eliza ✱ Beth

P.S. Congratulations on getting the part!

P.P.S. How is the friendship campaign coming?

P.P.P.S. I'll tell you about Kate's Kitchen some other time.

November 4, 10:06 P.M.

Dear Tara*Starr,

This is a whisper letter. If we were actually talking, I would have to whisper, since it's after ten o'clock at night and I'm supposed to be asleep. (My parents *always* know where I am at ten o'clock. I'm in bed.) So I'm writing this under the covers, with a flashlight, and I feel like I'm whispering to you.

Thank you so, so, so much for calling tonight. THANK YOU, THANK YOU, THANK YOU, THANK YOU, THANK YOU!!!! And please thank Barb again for me, okay? I can't believe you guys called as soon as you read my letter. I know the call was expensive, and I'm pretty sure you had to give some of your money to Barb to help pay for it. You know what? I'm going to pay you back. Is it okay to send cash through the mail? I'm not going to mail you coins, I'll just fold some bills into my next letter. I better not do it in this letter. Mom is still upset, and I don't want her to get suspicious of *any*thing right now.

Tara, do you know how good it felt to talk to you and Barb about what's going on with my parents? I've been feeling so lonely. And so alone. I feel like I don't have my family anymore, except for Emma. My parents are lost, at least to me. (There's always been a distance between my father and me, but now there's one between my mother and me too.) And I keep worrying about Emma. All this stuff is too big for me.

I've really been thinking about what Barb said. That I should go to my guidance counselor. But I'm not sure. You know how Mom feels about keeping things in the family.

Well, now I guess I better tell you what happened after Mom came into the kitchen and caught me on the phone with you and Barb. First of all, you should know that she wasn't upset because I was talking to you. (You know my mom likes you. And my father doesn't dislike you *that* much. Mom was upset because she heard me telling you what she considers private family business. She believes that family business should stay in the family. That's the guidance counselor problem. She was also upset because it was after dinner and Dad hadn't come home yet, so we'd eaten without him.

So guess what I did after Mom made me get off the phone. I don't think you'll believe this, but I asked Mom if she and Dad are getting a divorce. I mean, I just asked her straight out. I said, "Mom, are you and Dad getting a divorce?" I was really proud of myself for asking, but the result was kind of disappointing.

Mom said, "No, that's not what's going on."

So I said, "Is Dad having an affair?"

And here Mom got *really* upset. She said, "That sounds like something Tara would say." And then she cried.

So then I said, "Mom, please. Just tell me what's going on. *Please*."

And Mom sighed. "It's between grown-ups."

At least I asked.

I can hear footsteps in the hallway now, so I better end this letter and turn off the flashlight before I get caught.

I think maybe Dad just came home.

Love,

*Eliza*Beth*

P.S. Thank you again for calling. It was so great to talk to you in person. I really miss you, Tara. (Barb too.) You're my best friend and always will be.

P.P.S. You know what makes me happy? We started a poetry unit in English, and we're writing our own poetry. Even when I'm feeling my saddest, just thinking about my poems makes me feel better.

November 4, 10:10 P.M.

Dear Eliza*Beth,

I'm writing this immediately after your mom made you get off the phone.

Yikes . . . I feel so bad for you.

I can't believe that I used to think that your life was so easy.

Now your life seems like a nightmare!!!!!!!!!!!!!!!!!!!!

I wish that I had a magic wand to make it all better.

When we hung up, I cried. Did you?

Barb hugged me.

I wish she could have hugged you too.

Now I'm in my room, writing to you, using the special pen you gave me as a going-away present.

Oops — Barb's just come in to remind me that I've got to finish up my homework now so that my grades are good enough to be in the play. . . . Plus, I've got to get to school early tomorrow to meet with some of the kids and rehearse.

Let me know what's happening. I'm so worried about what's going on at your house.

Love,

Tara Starr

P.S. Luke just came into my room to make sure that I was doing my homework. (Do you believe how my parents are finally acting so grown-up and par-ently?) Anyway, he sends his love and hopes that things get better for you real soon.

P.P.S. I hope you don't mind that I'm talking about how parently my parents are becoming while yours are falling to pieces. It's all so weird, isn't it?

November 8

DEAR ELIZA*BETH,

I JUST READ YOUR "WHISPER" LETTER . . . .
. . . . AND . . . . THIS IS A "SHOUT"
LETTER!

TO ANSWER YOU:

1. YOU'RE WELCOME ABOUT OUR PHONE
CALL. I ONLY WISH THAT MY FAMILY HAD
ENOUGH MONEY TO CALL YOU EVERY
DAY . . . EVERY HOUR . . . EVERY MINUTE.

2. YOUR MOM IS SOOOOOOOOOO WRONG. (I HOPE THAT YOU DON'T MIND MY SAYING THAT, BUT SHE IS. . . . SOOOOOOOO WRONG.) YOU REALLY SHOULD GO TO YOUR GUIDANCE COUN-SELOR . . . OR ONE OF THE TEACHERS. (IS THERE ANYONE THERE YOU TRUST?) WHY DON'T YOU TRY TO BE FRIENDS WITH SOME OF THE KIDS WE HUNG AROUND WITH LAST YEAR? . . . AT LEAST THAT WAY YOU WOULD HAVE OTHER PLACES TO GO TO, TO GET OUT OF YOUR HOUSE SOMETIME. DOESN'T EMMA HAVE SOME FRIENDS THAT SHE CAN HAVE PLAY DATES WITH SO THAT YOU DON'T HAVE TO WATCH HER ALL THE TIME? YIKES!

3. PLEASE DON'T SAY THAT YOUR FATHER DOESN'T "DISLIKE ME***THAT MUCH***" YOU KNOW HE DOES . . . AND HE DOESN'T LIKE MY PARENTS EITHER. REMEMBER THAT TIME HE KEPT TALKING ABOUT HOW YOUNG MY PARENTS WERE, HOW THEY SHOULD HAVE "WAITED," HOW HE HOPED

THAT I WASN'T GOING TO HAVE THE SAME "PROBLEM" THAT THEY HAD. . . . YOU KNOW THAT HE DOESN'T APPROVE . . . THAT HE'S FIGURED OUT THAT MY PARENTS GOT MARRIED BECAUSE I WAS "ON THE WAY . . . GOING TO BE BORN." HE MADE IT SOUND LIKE I WAS THE "PROBLEM." SO ANYWAY, YIKES! . . . YOU DON'T HAVE TO PRETEND THAT YOUR FATHER LIKES ME. PLEASE DON'T PRETEND WITH ME . . . YOU HAVE TO DO THAT TOO MUCH IN YOUR HOUSE.

4. (I've decided to stop "shouting," to go back to regular writing with large and SMALL letters.) I'm glad that you like your poetry unit. I'm glad that something in your life isn't so awful.

Write back fast and let me know what's happening. I'm worried about you.

Love,

Tara Starr

P.S. You may have noticed that I've started saying "Yikes!" That's what the kids here in the drama group say a lot. They also say "Zounds," so I guess I've started saying that too. I've taught them "Gad-zooks." . . . Remember how we always used to say that? Anyway, maybe you would like to start saying "Yikes" and "Zounds" so that you can feel part of this group too. . . . You know, Eliza*Beth, some of them are really nice . . . and you'd like them . . . and I know they would like you too.

November 11, 4:22 P.M.

Dear Tara*Starr,

I got both your letters — the one you wrote after our phone call, and the one you wrote after you read my whisper letter. I sort of feel like writing a SHOUT letter back to you, but I'm too tired to play around with the shift key so much.

I'm watching Emma again while Mom is at Kate's Kitchen. I *like* taking care of Emma.

I know I didn't get around to telling you how Kate's Kitchen works, so I'll do it now. It's this organization that collects food (and also diapers, baby supplies, soap, shampoo, and stuff) and then donates the things to anyone who needs them. People can come to Kate's Kitchen and pick out the things they need, or volunteers like my mom can put together baskets for people who are too old or too sick to leave their houses. Some people get their meals delivered *every day.* And on holidays, Kate's Kitchen serves turkey dinners. It's kind of neat. I helped out once. I might go back. I can see why my mom likes working there.

Our poetry unit is SO COOL. I love it. It's the best thing about my life. I write poems all the time and I keep them in notebooks. Here's a poem I wrote this morning right after my alarm clock went off:

Time is a never ending thing.
It makes the clocks tick
And the church bells ring.
O Time! is a never ending thing.

Do you like it?

Your drama group sounds really great. The kids sound great too. Are they your new friends? I know you have to make new friends, but . . . I'm a little jealous. I can't help it. I liked it when we were best friends who saw each other every day. Maybe I'll start saying "Yikes" and "Zounds," but not yet. It doesn't feel right. I mean, it doesn't feel comfortable.

Just a sec. Emma is here and she wants a juice box. Okay, I'm back.

Well, whatever is going on with my parents has to do with Dad's job. I know that for sure now. (I guess he really has been at the office all those late nights.) I know this because the last few evenings Mom has called Dad at the office and they have all these conversations about his boss, his company, his job, what went on that day. And she keeps asking him if "anything happened." She sounds really nervous. And Dad has been coming home earlier (like around 9:00), and he seems nervous too. Then he and Mom just talk some more about his work. I am expected to go to bed quietly and not bother them.

Wait, here's Emma again. This time she wants to write something *on the computer*, which should be interesting.

hp Usmlrrd@@@@@ nsffiz somymp noh yhomh *NTPMC* NP,NRTD 07 USU

VVVVVVVVVVVVVVVVVVVVVVVVVVVVVVVVVV
VVVVVVVV

I just asked Emma what this means and she said, "Hi, Tara Starr! I miss you. Can you come over sometime? On Halloween I got candy and a quarter."

I better go. I have homework. I'll write again soon.

Love,

Eliza✱Beth

P.S. Hey, maybe now that your parents are all adult and responsible they'll let you get a *pet*!!!!!

November 15

Dear Eliza*Beth,

Yikes! Zounds! Egad!

It sounds *really* hard at your house.

Here's what I think:

1. Maybe your mom should stop spending so much time at Kate's Kitchen and take care of her own kids.

2. I'm glad that you are happy writing poetry. I was beginning to worry that there was nothing to make you happy. About your poem. It's

very nice. You know that I like poetry that doesn't rhyme, but your poem is very nice.

3. Double yikes! It sounds really bad about your dad's job. I know what it's like to worry about whether your father's going to have work. Remember how Luke was always changing jobs — or not working — and money was such a problem? . . . Oh, Eliza*Beth, do you think you're going to have to worry about money — about where you're going to live. . . . Whether the debt collectors are going to call. (I remember when it was like that for us.) . . . Oh, well, your family is so different from how mine used to be. I bet that they have lots of savings. (By the way — yesterday Luke said that we've saved enough to buy the front door to a house and maybe one room. (Down payment, not owning!!!)

4. Tell Emma I love her, and if I had a computer my message to her would be x qlrv jxa, guu.*

* That means I love you too.

5. I can't believe that you mentioned a *pet*. Just yesterday, Barb asked how I felt about having a baby brother or sister. Before I had a chance to say anything (well, actually I did fall on the floor and clutch my heart as if I was dying) Barb said, "Well, it's just a thought. Maybe we should get a puppy or a Venus fly-trap instead. . . ." I'm not sure if it was a joke or what.

6. About my friends — please don't be jealous. There's a lot that I want to tell you, but I'm not sure if I should, because you already feel so bad.

Well, gotta go.
Play practice . . . and then I've go *so* much homework. (Don't you think teachers should "cut some slack" for people in plays?!)

As always,

Tara Starr

November 19

Dear Tara*Starr,

A baby? *A BABY*??!!! Are you kidding me? Did Barb mean that? Oh, you have to find out. That is too exciting! That is the best, best news!!! Tara, you would like to have a little brother or sister. You know you would. Think how much you like Emma. And think what an incredible big sister you

November 20 10:07 P.M.

Dear Tara*Starr,

I never got to finish the letter I started yesterday.

I was *so* excited about the baby . . . and then Dad came home from work. He got home at five. And guess what. He was downsized. That means fired, although Dad says it isn't quite the same thing. Something happened at his company (Dad tried to explain it to me, but I didn't really understand), and they downsized forty of the top executives. *Forty.* And right before Thanksgiving. Dad has worked at Data-Pro for seventeen years. Since before he and Mom got married.

I said to Dad, "Well, you'll just have to get another job. What about the Help Wanted pages in the newspaper?"

And he said, "Honey, first of all they don't list quarter-of-a-million-dollar-a-year jobs in the Help Wanted pages." (I didn't know he earned a quarter of a million dollars a year. That's a fortune.) "And second, right now there are thirty-nine other people at my level — just from Data-Pro — all out there looking for the same kind of job I'd want. And there are not a lot of jobs available."

I hadn't thought of that, but I said, "Dad, a quarter of a million dollars a year. At least we have a huge savings account." (I was remembering what you'd said in your letter.) "Maybe you could even retire early. That would be fun." And that was when Dad shook his head, turned away, and left the room. I think there are things going on that I don't know about yet.

Dad fixed himself a drink with vodka in it — actually I think it might have been just vodka poured over ice cubes — and then he and Mom went into the living room to talk.

I overheard them. I knew they didn't want Emma and me in the living room, so I took Emma into the den. I told her I would read her a story, but instead I made her look at picture books while I tried to hear Mom and Dad. Dad said something about a package. (Do they give going-away presents to people they fire?) He said we could use the package to build up our savings account again. But Mom said well then what would we live on?

What would we *live* on? Tara, we are not poor. I must be missing something.

By bedtime last night, Emma knew something was wrong, and she was upset. I told her I would write a special poem for her. Since we are learning about haiku, this is what I wrote:

Little gray kitten

in a big brown shoe. Two tongues —

only one so pink.

Emma liked the idea of a kitten sitting in a shoe, but she didn't know that shoes have tongues, so the inner meaning was lost on her. Still . . . she went to bed happy.

I'll keep you posted.

How's the play? How are Barb and Luke?

ASK BARB ABOUT THE BABY, OKAY?

Zounds, it's after ten-thirty, so I better go to bed.

I miss you.

Love,

Eliza Beth

November 23

Dear Eliza*Beth,

Zounds! Zounds! Zounds!

A million times Zounds!

I don't know what to say.

Your news is soooooooo awful!

When I got up this morning (I overslept), Barb told me that there was a letter from you. (She always leaves your letters on the kitchen table — but last night I got in so late and I was sooooo tired that I didn't see the letter. . . . I can't believe that the FIRST time I don't come home and immediately check to see if a letter has arrived, not only has one arrived but it's got the *most awful news*.)

Please forgive me for not reading it sooner but yesterday was soooo busy. . . . First, I had detention for talking to Candace — she plays one of my sisters in the play. . . . Then some of the kids went to Mickey D's for dinner. (That's what they call McDonald's here.) Then there was play practice, which ran overtime because some of us can't remember our lines. Then Alex's father drove Alex and me home. (Have I mentioned he's got the bluest eyes? I mean Alex, not his father.)

Oh, Eliza*Beth — As soon as I got into study hall, I read your letter (hiding it in my science book). I was stunned!!!!! And if I'm feeling like this, I can't even imagine what you're feeling like. . . . Uh-oh! Mrs. Cross, my study hall teacher, is threatening to check to see that we're all really doing our schoolwork. (Just because a few kids keep whispering, passing notes, or playing battleship.) . . . It figures that someone named Mrs. Cross would be in a lousy mood most of the time. (Think about this: If Mrs. Cross's twin sister married Mr. Cross's twin brother, would they be double-crossed?)

I'd better stop writing now. . . . I'll mail this letter between dinner at Mickey D's and play practice.

Love and worry,

*Tara*Starr*

P.S. LONGER LETTER LATER

Dear Eliza*Beth,

This letter is written later (the night of the day I read about your dad getting fired).

Barb and I just had a long talk.

Here are some questions for you.

1. Is it all right for us to call you or will your father go ballistic?

2. Do you want to come here for Thanksgiv-ing? Barb & Luke said that we could use some

of our savings to help you pay for the plane ticket. (I'll give up those dinners at Mickey D's.)

3. Have you found someone there to talk to — a teacher, a counselor?

4. Does Emma understand what's happening?

5. Is your mom still so upset?

6. Will your mom stop volunteering at Kate's Kitchen and get a job?

7. Did you find out what a "package" is? Barb says that it's the money and benefits that some executives get when they're fired. She says that only "big deals" get a package, that regular people like her and Luke wouldn't get $, they would just get a pink slip (and we're not talking lingerie).

8. Are you okay?????????

9. Can you tell me what I can do to help you?

Love,

Tara*Starr

P.S. Will you be very disappointed if I tell you that Barb is just *thinking* about having a baby, that she and Luke aren't planning — but they are "continuing to practice" so that they don't forget how babies are made. (She is sooooo embarrassing sometimes.)

Eliza*Beth — Should I be talking about and joking about what's going on in my life, with my family, with my friends? I just don't know what to do — I don't know if I should tell you about the kids here. (I've been writing about some of the kids to let you know about them — but now I don't know if I should send that to you. What do you think?)

P.P.S. About your haiku — You should tell Emma that shoes and kittens not only have tongues but souls (soles).

P.P.P.S. (or is that P.S.S.S.) I really wish you were here.

November 27, 2:15 P.M.

Dear Tara*Starr,

Well, it's the day after Thanksgiving, and I just got your letters. I guess we both know I couldn't have come for Thanksgiving, even if I had gotten the letters in time. But I really, really, REALLY appreciate that you invited me. And I especially appreciate that Barb and Luke said you guys could use some of your savings to help pay for the plane ticket — at the exact time when you are saving for a house and probably need the money to make a down payment on your *back* door. You know what? If I *had* been allowed to visit you for Thanksgiving I think I *might* have needed to borrow some money. I'm still trying to figure out all the financial stuff. (Financial — a fancy word for money that my parents use about a thousand times an hour.) But this is the main thing: I think we are in Very Big Trouble. I don't quite know what happened, but somehow Mom and Dad didn't *save* much of the money Dad earned. Mom keeps reminding Dad that he bought a house he couldn't afford, and that all of our money goes into upkeep. By "upkeep" I think Mom means paying Jeannemarie, Martha, the gardeners, the decorator, the pool people, and stuff. Plus — and I *know* I am not supposed to tell you this, so please don't even tell Barb and Luke — I found out that our house cost six hundred *thousand* dollars. Now a quarter of a million dollars doesn't sound like so much money. With hardly any savings, and no one earning money around here, how are we going to pay for *anything*? Dad is still paying for the *house*. Mom said we have a huge mortgage. Are we going to have to *move*?

Tara, when I think of these things my stomach starts to feel queasy. Speaking of stomachs (which made me think of food), guess what. Yesterday we had the annual family Thanksgiving. As usual, Dad had been planning it forever — 30 guests, an enormous turkey, and the fanciest dinner ever. Dad insisted that we have it, to keep up appearances for his family. We weren't allowed to tell them he had been fired. It's always important to Dad to show his family how well he's doing. And so we had a very stiff, strained, huge, expensive dinner, and Dad didn't tell his family what happened, and I don't know how he paid for everything.

Okay, let me answer the rest of your questions.

Yes, it's okay for you to call me. My dad won't go ballistic, although he might not actually be thrilled. Just remember two things. 1. Now that Dad isn't working, he's almost always at home and might answer the phone. 2. DO NOT MENTION ANY OF THE FINANCIAL STUFF I HAVE BEEN WRITING TO YOU ABOUT. IT IS A *BIG* FAMILY SECRET. I AM PRACTICALLY UNDER OATH NOT TO TALK ABOUT IT. However, I would really love to talk to you, or to you and Barb, again. I felt sooooo much better after your other call.

About Emma. No, she doesn't understand what's

happening. She knows something is going on and that it's not good, but she doesn't know what "fired" means, let alone understand financial things. All she knows is that Daddy is home all day now. At first she was really excited about that, but now she tries to steer clear of him. So do I. As you can imagine, he is not in the best mood. Today he hasn't even gotten dressed yet.

Yes, I think Mom is still upset. She could be upset because:

a) we don't have enough money.

b) Dad sits around at home all day.

c) Dad thinks he's not going to get another job.

d) we might not have a house to live in.

e) there seems to be plenty of money for deliveries from the liquor store.

f) she hates Data-Pro.

g) she's afraid.

I think the last answer is the most likely one. It covers everything. Plus . . . I'm afraid too. So I kind of know how she feels.

I don't know if Mom is going to stop volunteering at Kate's Kitchen. She goes there absolutely every day. She even went on Thanksgiving Day for a few hours. (In fact, I think maybe she's spent *more* time there since Dad got fired.) I don't know if she'll get a job. I know she wants one, but Dad still doesn't want her to work, especially not now. (He doesn't want people to think she *needs* to work.) I could ask her about it, but I really don't want to ask her about anything touchy right now.

I haven't found out anything more about the package. But what Barb said makes sense. If Dad got some money when he was fired, then that would explain why he said we could use the package to build up our savings account. I guess he meant we could use it to *start* a savings account. But then Mom's right — if we save that money, what will we live on???

Yes, I'm okay, I guess. I don't really know what to tell you. I feel scared and sad and I have no idea what's going to happen to us now. If Dad found another job, that would change everything. But can he get one that pays him a quarter of a million dollars? There aren't a lot of jobs like that around. He'll probably start looking on Monday, though. I'm just glad I have Emma and poetry and Mrs. Jackson (she's my English teacher). I *love* Mrs. Jackson. She is so cool.

What can you do to help? JUST KEEP WRITING!!! I look forward to your letters sooooo much. I check the mail every day, just in case. And if you and Barb call, that will be great.

Hey — tell Barb and Luke to stop practicing and start planning! I want you to have a little brother or sister. You don't know how great it will be.

Love,

Eliza ✶ *Beth*

P.S. Of course you should be talking about the play and your friends. I like knowing there's a different life going on, one that isn't mine. And right now yours seems kind of perfect.

Dec. 2

Dear Eliza*Beth,

Oh, Eliza*Beth.

Bad news.

Such bad news.

Your news was bad enough.

Now I've got to tell you more bad news. (A lot of bads!!!!! — and it's just beginning!!!!)

I rushed home right after school today (I forgot one of my costumes — you know *how* forgetful I can be) and there was your letter. Even though I was supposed to rush back to school, I stopped to read it and then I showed it to Barb, who was home with a stomach flu. After talking to her, I immediately called your house. Your father answered, and when I said, "May I please speak to Elizabeth?" (I was soooo careful to be polite) he said, "Who is this?" "Tara*Starr, sir," I replied. He said, in a kind of nasty, slurred voice, "About what do you want to talk to her?"

I didn't know what to say, so as usual, I tried to joke my way around it. "Girl stuff," I said.

He said, "You always were so silly. . . . Well, Elizabeth is not in right now."

When I asked when you would be back, he didn't say anything.

I think I heard the sound of ice cubes in a glass as he took a drink.

I repeated, "When will she be back?"

"I don't know," he yelled. He actually yelled at me. "Why don't you just stop bothering us?"

And then he hung up. He actually hung up on me.

I kept holding on to the phone and started crying. When I told Barb what happened, she took the phone from me, hung up, and then she hit the redial button.

Your father answered again.

He told her to mind her own business and said that he preferred that we not contact you, that I'm really not the type of friend he wants for his daughter, and that you could do so much better.

Barb got angry — and you know that even though she hardly ever gets really angry, when she does — it's major!!!!

Her voice got stone cold and she said to your father, "Our daughters are good for each other. *They* know the meaning of friendship and respect."

Then your dad said some bad words and hung up.

I'm scared.

Did he yell at you after we called?

Was he drunk?

Did he even tell you we called?

I hope this letter gets to you. I made the envelope look like it came from Karen "Barfola" Frank. (He always liked her.) You can tell him that she's moved away.

I've really got to go now. I'm going to be in deep trouble with my director for being so late to practice. Barb is going to drive me back to school and tell the director that there was/is a family emergency.

But first Barb wants to add something.

Love,

Tard*Starr

ELIZA*BETH, DEAR —

I want you to know that we're thinking about you. Please feel free to call us collect whenever you can. We'll accept the call.

And please — try to find someone there to talk to and help you.

Love,

Barb

December 7

Dear Tara*Starr,

Today is Pearl Harbor Day. This seems appropriate, since I feel a little like I'm in a war.

Thank you for your letter, and for Barb's note. I don't know what to say about my dad except that I'm sorry. (I *didn't* know you had called. Dad didn't tell me.) I'm sorry he was rude to you and Barb. I also feel sorry for *him.*

You probably did hear ice cubes in a glass when you were talking to him. They could have been in a glass of Pepsi or something, but I guess we both know

86

they were more likely in a drink. A *drink* drink. I can't ignore all the liquor that's been coming into the house. It used to be that Dad would have exactly one drink before dinner. Then over the summer he started having a drink before dinner and wine with dinner. In September he started having a drink before dinner, wine with dinner, and a few drinks after dinner. Now he drinks during the day too.

Yesterday Emma told me that Daddy scares her. He never hurts us or anything. That's not what I mean at all. But he seems like a different person when he drinks. Emma summed it up pretty well when she was getting ready for Miss Fine's this morning and referred to him as "the other Daddy."

You know what, though? I did one really good thing. I did it yesterday. (I knew you and Barb would be proud of me, but that's not why I did it.)

After Emma told me that Daddy scares her, I started thinking that I really do need to talk to someone about what's happening. I remembered that Barb suggested my guidance counselor, and even though Mr. Holtz has never been any help to me before (he's pretty useless), I decided to go see him. Maybe I just hadn't gone to him with a big enough problem.

When I got to the guidance office there were, like, seven kids in the waiting room. And the doors to the counselors' offices were all open. Of course, no kids were in Mr. Holtz's office, so he told me to come in right away. And then . . . he didn't close the door. I was sitting there, two inches away from the open door, and Karen Frank and these other kids were all right outside.

"So . . . what can I do you for?" said Mr. Holtz, and he laughed, like he just invented that question.

I glanced out in the waiting room. Then I looked at the door. It was propped open with a needlepoint-covered brick. A suit of clothes was hanging on the door, so I knew it would have to *stay* open. Tara, how could I tell Mr. Holtz about my dad and his job and the drinking and that we might not even have a house — when all those kids would overhear? My parents would kill me. Plus, Mr. Holtz was cleaning under his nails with a toothpick. So I just said, "Um, maybe I could make an appointment to talk about what classes to take next year?" And we did. (The appointment is in January.)

Then I left. I felt like crying. But while I was walking along, trying not to cry, I ran into Mrs. Jackson. I guess I looked upset because she asked what was wrong. I drew in a very deep breath, and I said, "Can I talk to you?"

She put her arm across my shoulders and said, "Sure. Let's go to my office."

As soon as we were in her office, she closed the door. And I blurted out, "My father got fired. He lost his job."

You know what? She said, "Oh, I'm sorry. My husband lost his job about six years ago. Things were tight for a few months, but he found another job by Christmas. That was one of our best Christmases ever."

Well, even though I hadn't told her about the drinking or the financial problems, I felt better. I asked Mrs. Jackson if I could talk to her every now and then, and she said yes! Isn't that good?

I better go. I'm going to mail this letter on my way to school instead of leaving it for Mom to mail. Dad might see it and . . . I don't know. It might not get mailed at all if he does see it.

How's the play going?

Is Barb pregnant yet? (Are you *sure* that was just the stomach flu she had?)

Love,

Eliza ✱ Beth

December 15

Dear Eliza*Beth,

I'm sorry that it's taken so long to answer your letter. I've been soooo busy (and I just don't know what to say to you anymore).

It does seem like you're in a war . . . and I feel like I'm reading about some foreign country while I'm in my safe classroom — and that what's going on is so far away and so unreal. But the difference is that I do know someone in that "foreign country" — and it's you!!!

You — Eliza*Beth, one of my best friends in the

entire world — and I don't know what to do, what to say.

I feel like I shouldn't tell you what's going on here — because it's gotten so happy and so good. (You should see the letters that I've written to you but ended up throwing away because they are all about the kids here, the school, the play, the parties, the fun.) It's not all perfect — it's not always been easy being the new kid — having my parents be so different, sooooo responsible — not Charents, but parents!!! But next to what's happening to you — it all seems so — I don't know — so happy — so too-small problems. You're the one in the war, with an alcoholic father, a mother who's gone AWOL (we studied that in history — that means "absent without leave"), impending poverty, a little sister who is terrified about the war and feels totally helpless, who depends on you. And when you try to get help from the people in power (The Guidance Counselor) there is no help — only a needlepoint doorstop. You are in a war!!!! It's soooo great that your English teacher is there. I just wish she could negotiate peace at your house — or at least a truce. (Maybe a Christmas truce — don't they do that in wars?)

Now, since you asked for news about Barb —
and the baby — actually about the non-baby. I
asked Barb — and she said that she's NOT pregnant.
Then she said, "Not yet. Your father and I are too
busy right now raising three children. You" (meaning me) "and us" (meaning them). "So we're not
ready."

Yikes . . . "Not yet." "Not ready." That means
they *are* thinking about it. I'm not sure I want a baby
brother or sister. Does that make me selfish? Does it
make me selfish because I'm having a good time and
you're not? (And that I don't think about your problems all the time? Somehow I think if I was the one
with trouble — you would be miserable all the time
to keep me company — Oh, Eliza*Beth — I worry
that I'm not a good enough friend.)

Love,

*Tara*Starr*

December 19

Dear Tara*Starr,

I just got your letter. It was waiting for me when I came home from school. (Mom puts your letters in my room now, if she's the one who takes in the mail, and she usually is. So you don't have to worry too much about whether I'll get them. I don't think I've missed a letter yet.) Anyway, before I forget — I mailed a package to you yesterday. It's your Christmas package. There are two things for you from me in it, and something for you from Emma. (She's really proud of it, by the way, so you have to make a big deal out of it after you open it.) Also, there's a little present for Barb in the package. Because she's been so nice to me. I'm afraid there isn't anything for Luke. I didn't exactly forget him. I just didn't know *what* to get him. Besides, I ran out of money.

You know what? I feel horrible. Not about Luke. About Christmas. Well, really about everything.

It's Christmas but it doesn't feel like it. We got a tree, and last weekend we decorated it. But the tree is crooked in the stand because Dad had three vodka drinks before he put it up. And then he fell asleep, so Mom put him to bed while Emma and I decorated the tree by ourselves. We didn't do a very good job.

Tara, I could go on and on about Christmas here, but I have to stop and say something. Do you know that in your letter you called me one of your best friends in the entire world? *One* of your best friends. ONE of them. I thought I was your *only* best friend. (You are *my* only best friend.) So who are all these other best friends you have?

And excuse me, but you called my father an alcoholic and said my mother has gone AWOL. I don't think either of those things is true. Dad just has a little drinking problem now, that's all. And my mother is doing her best. She needs to get out of the house sometimes, especially now that Dad's home all day. So maybe you could be a little kinder about them. At least about my mother.

So much is happening to me, Tara. I feel overwhelmed. So much is going on that I can't even get very angry at you. There's barely room for that inside me. You hurt my feelings. You really did. But I can't concentrate on that for too long, because of all the other stuff.

Most of the other stuff has to do with Christmas. Like I said, it doesn't feel like Christmas usually feels at my house. We put up that tree, but it might as well be someone else's. We're not doing *any* of our usual Christmas things. And Dad is just sitting around, watching soap operas in his bathrobe and not taking phone calls. (Also, he's busy not looking at the mail. He just throws away most of the things Mom hands him.)

Our house is dreary, and I haven't been to any Christmas parties or seen any of the kids. I just don't feel like being with them. The worst thing, though, is Emma. She *really* believes in Santa Claus and she is very excited. She came up with a list of toys. The list is about two feet long. She dictated it to me. She wants Barbies and a bicycle with training wheels, a dollhouse, this machine that makes fake fingernails, and that's only the beginning. There's no way Mom and Dad can get her much of anything, so Emma is going to be *so* disappointed. I've tried to help by saying that *I* don't want anything this year, but I have no idea what's going to happen. If Mom and Dad can't make house payments, they won't be able to spend money on something as frivolous (new vocab. word — look it up) as toys. I have $8.53 in cash right now. It's in my bureau drawer. But I have several hundred $$ in that savings account my grandparents opened for me. Mom and Dad have always said that's my money. They have also always told me I can't touch it. (It's to be saved, not spent.) And Dad keeps the passbook. But I know where it is, and tomorrow after school I am going to take $30 out of my account. I don't think my parents will notice that little amount. I figure $38.53 will be enough to buy Emma a Barbie, some Barbie clothes, and a few small toys. I won't have a penny left for other gifts, but I can make things for Mom and Dad, grandparents, etc. in the crafts room at school. The important thing is that

Emma will have presents from Santa. I don't want her to be disappointed on Christmas morning.

I better go. I'm so tired. I'm tired all the time. When am I going to feel like a human? Maybe I'll try to talk to Mrs. Jackson again.

Love,

*Eliza*Beth

P.S. Tara — PLEASE. TELL ME ABOUT YOU, THE PLAY, YOUR SCHOOL. Like I said before, I want to know what's going on. I want to know about someone else's life. I'm tired of mine. I want a little peek at something that's normal — a family without secrets. Tell me about Christmas with Barb and Luke, okay? Are you going to get a tree this year? Are you going to have Christmas dinner? (Remember the year you had McDonald's for Christmas dinner?) Did you get a present for your parents yet?

P.P.S. REMEMBER TO TELL EMMA HOW MUCH YOU LIKE HER PRESENT. She made it herself.

Christmas night

Dear Tara*Starr,

Well, Christmas is just about over. It's a little after 8:00. Mom is putting Emma to bed. Dad is downstairs, sitting in an armchair, staring into the fireplace. We had quite a day. You won't believe what happened (or what I'm wearing).

First, let me tell you that your package arrived — just in time. It came yesterday. On December 24th! When Emma saw the box and I told her it was from you, she got all excited. We opened it right away and

99

put the presents under the tree. A few things were already there. Presents from our aunts and uncles and grandparents. And one present each for Mom and Dad from me. (In the crafts room I made Dad a ceramic dog for his bureau. And I framed a picture I had cross-stitched for Mom.) I thought those were probably the only presents that would be under the tree, except for what I bought for Emma, so when Emma *begged* to open the gift from you early, I said no. I said it would be more fun to wait. (Since I knew "Santa" wasn't coming.) So we waited. And guess what. Tara, I am still so stunned by what happened that I almost don't know how to tell it to you.

I guess I'll just start at the beginning, which was last week. With the $38.53 I went to Value Town (remember when you and I used to go there?) and looked for all the best toy bargains. For $38.21, including tax, I got Emma a Barbie, a Barbie ball gown, some Barbie swimwear, a coloring book, a box of 64 crayons with a sharpener on the back, a package of stickers, a puzzle, and a little stuffed angel bear. Isn't that amazing? I walked around with a calculator so I could get as much as possible without overspending and then having to tell the cashier I didn't have enough $$ and would have to put something back. See? Our math skills do come in handy.

Later, I wrapped each present separately, so it would look as if Santa had been particularly generous. Then at 5:05 this morning I snuck downstairs with them. Well, guess what. Sometime between when I went to bed and 5:05 a *sleighful* of presents appeared under our tree. They must have been from Mom and Dad, I thought, but what could they be? I mean, there were so *many* of them. I left Emma's presents under the tree and ran back to bed. An hour and a half later, Emma woke up, and soon we were downstairs opening the presents. Here is the stunning part. Emma got every single thing on her list from the bicycle to the dollhouse to the fingernail machine.

And remember how I said I didn't want anything this year? Well, I guess because of that I didn't get as *many* presents as Emma did. But here is what I did get: a cashmere sweater, a camera, real pearl earrings, and (this is the *most* stunning part) a diamond bracelet. I am not kidding you, Tara. Dad bought me a *real diamond bracelet*. How do I know Dad bought it? Because I'm pretty sure he did all the shopping.

My clue is that the sweater doesn't fit, and Mom would never make that mistake. She always gets clothes for Emma and me that fit perfectly. But the new sweater is too small. Plus, Mom looked really pained while Emma and I opened all our stuff. *Plus,* Dad gave her emerald earrings and a matching emerald necklace. PLUS, Mom didn't give Dad anything. I think maybe she assumed that they wouldn't give each other presents this year, which of course would make sense.

I am so confused. You know I'm not good at guessing how much stuff costs, but, well, even if I just try to figure the cost of the jewelry and the watch, don't you think Dad must have spent at least $5,000? Maybe $10,000? And that doesn't include the sweater, the camera, or all the toys. I bet Emma's toys cost another $1,000. I have *totally* misunderstood what's going on around here, or — Well, I don't know what the "or" could be. Is my father crazy? Is he stealing? Did he just spend the last penny we have?

You know what? Dad looked kind of proud of himself today (which is another reason I know he bought all the presents) but he also looked nervous.

Or scared or something. Do you think it's possible he *charged* everything? On credit cards? Can you do that? I mean, can you charge $10,000 worth of stuff? What happens when you can't pay the credit card companies? Do they come take the stuff away from you? WHAT HAS MY FATHER DONE?

Mom looks afraid and I feel so bad for her.

I wonder if I could give my presents back to the stores and then put the money in my bank account to give to Mom later, when we need it. But I don't know how to do that. I don't even know what stores the gifts came from.

You know what I do know? I know that I need to have a Very Big Talk with Mom soon. She thinks she's protecting me by not telling me more about what's going on, but I'll just have to tell her how much I've already figured out. And how scared I am. So when the time seems right I am going to talk to her. I think it will be okay.

Please write to me, Tara. I know I got a little mad in my last letter. About being *one* of your best friends. And because you're going overboard about my parents. But you're still my friend and I want to hear from you. I REALLY do want to know about your new friends and the play and school. And the Charents. Everything.

Did you like the presents from Emma and me? (Emma is dying to know.) Oh, and I *love* the sweater you sent! It's perfect! It fits. (It doesn't have to be dry cleaned.)

Merry Christmas, Tara.

Love,

Eliza✶Beth

P.S. I promise I'll stop asking about Barb and the baby.

P.P.S. Guess what Emma's *favorite* present was. The box of crayons. She likes the sharpener.

Dear Eliza*Beth,

I just received your letter. Wow!!!!!!!!!!!! First, I want to thank you for your presents. I know how hard you worked on them. The books are wonderful. The blank one, for me to do creative writing in, has a terrific cover. (You know how much I love rainbows.) I will write in it as soon as I have time, when the play is finished. . . . And the book with the pictures of the kittens on the cover, the one filled with your poetry, took so much work. The poetry is really amazing!!! Gadzooks!!! You sure have been writing a lot lately. (I only wish that it was happier.) Please tell Emma that I LOVE the yarn octopus that she made. (Don't tell her that one of the wiggly eyes fell off.) Tell her that I named it Emmapuss. (Emmapus sounded too gross!!!!) Barb loves her present. It must have taken you ages to cross-stitch that house with HOME SWEET HOME under it. Barb said that it was so thoughtful of you to make it for our future home (owned). We now have it hung up in this apartment (rented) and think of you whenever we look at it. (You know that we think of you at other times too.)

Christmas this year was wonderful. (I wish that yours was better.) I got clothes, especially this one dress that I've been craving to wear to the New Year's Eve party. I also got some scarves (one with glitter), a pair of glitter socks, and a pair of beaded sneakers . . . also some really cool earrings (one pair of dream catchers, one of peacock feathers, one frowny face — to make fun of the smiley face ones). My other big present was that Barb and Luke had given me some money early so I could buy those presents for you and Emma. (That made me so happy. I can baby-sit and stuff once the play is over but until then I'm low on money.) Barb and Luke took the money that they would have used on presents for each other and put it in their special "house savings account" . . . and there is no "baby savings account"!!!! I really don't think that's going to happen. Anyway, I like being an only child. Oh . . . and when they went out shopping for my presents, they saw and bought a pair of candlesticks. (They each wrapped and gave one to the other, along with candles.) They're putting the candlesticks away until we get a house and then we'll light the candles to celebrate.

As for your Christmas . . . gadzooks!!!!!! Are you sure that the jewels are real? Maybe now that your dad is home all day, he's been watching one of those television shopping stations and he bought the make-believe stuff. (Even that isn't always inexpensive.)

I can't figure out your finances either. I really did think your family was going to need food stamps. (Remember when my family needed them? It was, okay, a little embarrassing, but they really helped.) Somehow (don't get angry when I say this), I can't visualize your mom in the grocery line, wearing that jewelry and paying with food stamps. Your family must have money saved. (You know that your father and I don't like each other, but I don't think he's a thief.) I remember that you said your father grew up poor, but your mom's family has lots of money (don't they?) and maybe they gave your family some of it.

It *is* a good idea to talk to your mom about this . . . and maybe she'll know how to return some of the stuff. (A diamond bracelet for someone our age seems weird.)

Personally, I think you should return the Barbie stuff. You know Barbies make me puke.

As for my life, you asked, so I'll tell you. IT'S REALLY REALLY GOOD. (I wish your life was too.) The play is fun. I've met soooooo many people because of it. One of them is Hannah. (She's my Ohio best friend. You'd like her. She's fun. She's smart. She wants to be a writer — and an actress.) I love that her name spelled backward is the same as when it's spelled forward, a palindrome. I started calling her Pal Indrome. Now it's her new nickname. Everyone in our group calls her "Pal."

There are a lot of other kids that I'll tell you about

in another letter. Right now I want to talk about ALEX. Remember him???? He's now my BOY-FRIEND!!!! (Remember how we always talked about what it would be like to have a boyfriend? Well, it's great.) He's so much fun . . . he's soooooooo cute . . . and he's a really good kisser. (I found that out when we went to the movies last week.)

Of course the only other boy I ever kissed was Dwight Jones (in the third grade . . . he slugged me after I kissed him . . . that certainly stopped me for a long time!!!!). Well, this time I got kissed first, and it sure was nice (even though my lip got a little scratched by his braces once).

Oh, Eliza*Beth . . . I only wish you could be as happy as I am right now. . . . I also wish we could see each other every day like we used to be able to do. There's no one in the world who knows me as well . . . who knows what my life has always been like. . . . In some ways that's good. Here no one knows about my family's really poor, really rough times. You know more about me than anyone else does . . . only with you could I really talk about the changes, how even though they are so good — sometimes I'm scared that they'll go away.

I miss you.

I wish you a happy new year (well, at least a happier one).

Love,

Tara Starr

Elizabeth

January 6

Dear Tara*Starr,

What New Year's Eve party? Did you go to it with Alex? Was he your date? Were Hannah and your other friends there? Where was the party? At school? At someone's house? I want to know EVERYTHING. Especially whether Alex kissed you at midnight, with streamers and confetti showering down on you, and horns blowing. That is how I always dream of New Year's Eve. Kissing someone at midnight with con-fetti floating onto our hair and shoulders.

Guess how I spent New Year's Eve. At home with

Emma. I baby-sat. Dad wanted Martha or someone to come stay with us while he and Mom went to this big fancy party, but I had gotten it into my head to see the new year in with Emma. Just the two of us. When I said that I really, really, really wanted to baby-sit, Mom looked kind of relieved and said okay right away. It's funny — Mom's trying to save five dollars here, twenty dollars there, while Dad's out buying jewels. (They *are* real jewels, Tara. I'll tell you more about that later.)

Two interesting things happened at New Year's — one on New Year's Eve, one on New Year's Day. Here's what happened on New Year's Eve: Mom and Dad left around 8:00 ALL DRESSED UP. Dad was wearing his tux, and Mom was wearing a long gown and the emerald jewelry Dad gave her for Christmas. I watched Mom get ready for the party. I was trying to decide if it was a good time to talk to her but decided it wasn't, so I just sat on the bed and watched her put on her makeup and stuff. I saw her reach into the jewelry box for the emerald necklace and earrings, take them out, look at them, put them back, then take them out again and put them on, like she didn't really want to wear them. Anyway, Mom and Dad finally left, and Emma and I did a little dance around the living room. We were on our own, and even Emma had permission to stay up until midnight. She was desperately excited about this. So guess what time she fell asleep. 9:25 P.M. And guess what I did between then and waiting for the ball to drop at midnight. First I read a little, then I worked on a new cross-stitch project, and then (you won't believe this) I looked through my father's desk. I couldn't help myself. Guess what I found. A batch of notices from companies with names like North Radcliffe Agency and Turner-Whitman Services. These are collection agencies. Three of the envelopes had been opened, so I pulled out the letters. Each one demanded the payment of a bill. I don't know what got into me, but the fourth envelope was still sealed — and I steamed it open. The letter inside was just like the other three. Really mean sounding, like Dad will be in A LOT of trouble if he doesn't pay the bills. I resealed the envelope with a very thin layer of Elmer's glue. I hope Dad won't be able to figure out what I did, but you know what I think? If he does figure it out, I don't care, because it's nowhere near as bad as what Dad has done. Dad is buying stuff he can't afford, and then he isn't paying for it. You said Dad isn't a thief, Tara, but I think what he's doing is the same as stealing.

That was New Year's Eve. On New Year's Day I talked to Mom. My New Year's resolution is to speak up more, at least in my family. (I wonder where I got that idea.) So after lunch, while Dad was out some-where and Emma was playing with her Barbies, I said, "Mom, I have to talk to you. It's really impor-tant."

Mom was going through some papers at her desk, but she said, "Okay, honey."

And then, guess what. I told her *everything* — everything I have overheard about our finances (and I did not apologize for eavesdropping), about the Christmas presents (the ones I bought, and how sur-prised I was by the ones *Dad* bought), about finding those letters last night, everything. Finally, I just said, "I'm so confused. Can't you please tell me what's go-ing on?"

Mom sighed, but she didn't turn away or start to cry. She said, "Elizabeth, you are old enough. You do have a right to know what's going on."

Tara, it turns out my dad sort of has a problem,

and it isn't the drinking, although I guess that doesn't help. Mom said that Dad just cannot bear to admit to himself or anyone else that he's lost his job and that we are in bad shape. Bad financial shape, I mean. He's trying to pretend that nothing has changed, to show everyone we still have money. She said that even when we *did* have money he overspent. There are always bills he's late paying. Mom told me how Dad bought the Christmas presents. (That's when she told me the jewels are real.) He CHARGED them. And he won't be able to pay the credit card bills when they come in. (The letters I found last night are about OTHER bills he can't pay.)

Mom was going to tell me more — about our savings and Dad's package and stuff — but Dad came back just then. When we heard the car pull into the garage, Mom and I looked at each other.

"We'll have to finish this discussion another time," said Mom.

"Okay. As soon as possible," I said. I said it very firmly.

Mom looked surprised, but all she said was, "Yes, definitely. The next time your father is out, okay?"

"Okay."

I do not know where this firmness is coming from. Is it coming from anger? I am very mad at Dad.

Love,

Eliza Beth

P.S. Of course a diamond bracelet is a weird present for someone our age. Actually, it's stupid. Where am I supposed to wear it? To school? What would I do with it during gym class? For now I have left it in the box it came in. I have never taken it out (I haven't tried it on). I figure when we need money, I'll just give the box to Mom and she can turn it in at the jewelry store for cash. She must know where it came from, and all grown-ups know how to return merchandise.

January 13

Dear Eliza*Beth,

I am sooooooooo glad that you finally talked to your mom.

Wow ——— Your dad really needs to wake up and smell the stinkweeds! He sounds out of control!!!!!!! I remember once when my parents maxed out on their credit card. Of course, they only had one and they probably couldn't charge as much on it as your dad can spend on his cards. Luke had lost one of his jobs and they borrowed on their card and then charged at the grocery store. The collection letters were really bad . . . and then the phone calls started. (Have you gotten any of the phone calls yet? . . . Pretty awful!!) Then Luke got a new job, but by that time they were really in debt and couldn't figure out what to do. So they went to a special place that helps people learn how to budget, how to live without credit cards, and how to pay off debts. Maybe your parents should go to one of those places. If you want, I can ask my parents for the phone number.

More about my parents. . . . For their New Year's resolutions, they've decided to go to college. (They will each take one class each semester at the community college and then eventually transfer to the state college. They'll keep their jobs and go to school at night. We tried to figure it out. They'll probably graduate from college when I do!!!!!!!

* * * * * * *NOW FOR THE REALLY BIG NEWS . . . THE INFORMATION THAT YOU'VE REQUESTED* * * *
* *

NEW YEAR'S EVE . . . NEW YEAR'S EVE . . . NEW YEAR'S EVE . . .

THE DRESS — MY FIRST REALLY GROWN-UP ONE . . . black, long, scoop neck. (Barb only let me buy it because we could cut it shorter after New Year's and I could wear it as a regular dress for special occasions.) Luke looked at me when I came downstairs, then he groaned and said, "My little girl is growing up too fast, and I want that scoop neck covered with a scarf, a shawl, a suit of armor." I think he's having trouble with the fact that I've actually got boobs now. (Remember when we stuck your mom's shoulder pads on our chests and pretended that we had breasts?) I wore my peacock feather earrings, painted my nails purple with silver sparkles, and wore my glitter Doc Martens. (I got them on sale.)

THE PLACE . . . Glory and Tory Hancock's house. Oh, Elizabeth . . . they're twins . . . identical twins . . . brown hair, blue eyes. You can tell them apart because Glory has a scar over her left eyebrow. (She got it falling off a swing.) And you'll never believe this. . . . Their mother is also a twin AND her twin lives next door with her twin sons (Jerry and Terry Mallowen, who are also in our seventh-grade class). The husbands in these two families are not twins . . . that would have been too weird for words!!!!!!! Anyway, the party was held at the

Hancocks' house and then after the party was over all of the girls had a pajama party at the Hancocks' and the boys stayed over at the Mallowens'. That way no one had to be in cars late on New Year's Eve.

The party was fun . . . but do you know what???? I really don't understand boys. My parents dropped Hannah and me off at the party. (Then they went back home, where they spent the evening alone together.) When we got there, Alex was already at the party. He waved to me but kept right on talking to the other boys from the class. For the first hour all of the boys stayed on one side, playing Nerf football, and all of the girls kept admiring what each of us was wearing and talking about how all of the boys were being so immature playing Nerf football. Finally, I went over and started playing Nerf football with the boys. Soon everyone was playing.

Then Glory put on some CDs and we made up a new dance, "The Nerf." It was fun!!!!!! Afterward we all sat around, ate pizza, and watched videos. And yes, Alex sat next to me . . . and yes, he kissed me a couple of times . . . but I think he was more interested in putting Fritos and Chee-tos down his best friend's shirt. (His best friend is Martin, who's "going

out" with Hannah.) At midnight, there was no con-
fetti. Some of the guys did throw the Fritos and
Chee-tos up in the air . . . and then they tried to
catch them in their mouths.

So Alex and I did kiss each other at 12:08 . . . but
it was sort of gross because the Chee-to in his mouth
ended up in my mouth.

Somehow I don't think that seventh-grade boys
are all that interested in romance.

Well, that's my report.

Love,

Tara Starr

January 20

Dear Tara*Starr,

I can't believe your parents are going back to school! At their age. That is so cool. They will probably always be the oldest in their classes.

And Tara, your New Year's Eve sounds—Well, I was going to say dreamy, but dreamy is not exactly the word I would use to describe getting someone else's spitty Chee-to in your mouth. It does sound like a lot of fun, though. And your dress sounds beautiful, more like a gown. What did Hannah (Pal) wear?

Did she have a gown too? Did you two get dressed together and fix each other's hair and everything?

Guess what. Mom kept her promise. The next time she and I were alone in the house (which was a few days later), she said, "Elizabeth? Would you like to finish our discussion now?"

And I said, "Actually, I would like to *continue* it, but I don't want to finish it. I want us to *keep* talking about things. Is that okay?"

Mom hesitated just a little, but she smiled and said, "That's fine." She looked at me hard then. Not in a hard *way,* she just really studied me. Finally, she kind of frowned and said, "When did you get so grown-up, honey?"

"In the last few months," I said. I meant that seriously, but Mom laughed. (Not meanly, though.) "No, really," I said. "It's taken awhile, but I'm starting to figure out about Dad. And I feel like it really is making me grown up. Last year I didn't even know about collection agencies. Now I know what they are. And I know what they mean to someone like Dad. But Mom, can you tell me about our savings? That's confusing me. We must have savings. Right?"

Mom sighed. She said, "Honey, I don't want you to have to worry about these things."

I said, "I know. But now I know about them, sort of, and I'll feel better if you just tell me what's *really* going on. Because the things I can make up to worry about are probably worse than the truth."

So Mom said, "All right. This is what is really going on. We have almost no savings. We never have. Your father earned a very high salary for quite some time. High enough to be able to afford payments on this house, which is not paid off, but at least we have just the one, original mortgage. High enough to afford to pay Martha and Jeannemarie and the gardeners and the pool people. High enough to buy expensive cars and clothes and jewelry and gifts, and to give fancy parties and to take extravagant vacations. But —"

"But he spent all our money?" I guessed. "He never saved any?"

"Hardly any," replied Mom. "And what he did save is already gone."

"What about the package?" I asked. (And you know what? I almost laughed then because "package" made me think of "pink slip" and that made me think of what you said about lingerie.)

"The package comes in installments and will barely cover the mortgage on the house," said Mom. "We can either pay the mortgage each month or pay our other bills, including, for instance, grocery bills." Mom paused. "Your father did receive a lump sum of money at the time he was fired, but I convinced him to use that to pay some of the back bills. It covered most of them."

"How could he charge our Christmas presents?" I asked. I was surprised the credit card companies still let him use his cards.

Mom sighed. "He used a card he hasn't had any trouble with yet. But that company will be coming after us soon enough now."

"Mom, let's take my diamond bracelet back to the jewelry store. Please? It's kind of a wei — I mean, I like it, but where am I going to wear it?" I asked.

"Well, I guess we can do that, honey, but — and I hate to say this — the money would only be a drop in the bucket."

Mom was looking a little pale then, and I could

understand why. Even so, I asked the question I'd been dreading. "What are we going to do now?"

Mom let out the most enormous sigh. "I'm not sure, Elizabeth. Unless your father can find another very high-paying job very quickly, we will probably lose the house and quite a few of the things we own. We'll have to move to a smaller house with no Jeannemarie or Martha and live on a lot less money. I can't tell you specifically what's going to happen, though. It depends on so many things. We're just going to have to take things day by day."

"Can't somebody *lend* us some money?" I asked. I was starting to feel panicky.

Mom made a little face. "Well, no bank is going to lend us anything. That's for sure. And your father's family doesn't have any money."

"What about your parents?" I asked, thinking of Grandpa and Nana's house in Florida.

"They'll be able to help us out here and there," said Mom. "I mean, they certainly aren't going to let us starve. But they're not as wealthy as you might think. They've done very nicely financially, but a good chunk of their savings is tied up in the retirement community they moved to. Honestly, Elizabeth, if we want to preserve our *lifestyle,*" Mom said, "we'd need hundreds of thousands of dollars. Grandpa and Nana have some money, but nowhere near that much."

When I thought things over later — after Dad had come home and the talk had ended — I realized what Mom had been saying. That Grandpa and Nana can lend us or give us small amounts of money so that, just like Mom said, we won't actually *starve,* but that's about it.

Tara, you know what I was thinking about the other day? I don't know why, but I remembered the time we rode our bicycles to the mall and ate lunch at Chan's and then still had enough money to buy Cadbury eggs. It was almost Easter, and that huge Easter Bunny was walking around the mall, handing out bags of jelly beans to little kids. And even though we had our chocolate eggs, you went up to the Easter Bunny and said, "Flopsy, eggsactly what are you? A human bean? A jelly bean? Or a bunny bean? What if my friend and I tell you a hare-raising tail? Will you give us some of your candy?" And then he called you a Punster and you called him The Bunster, so he gave us the candy. I was just remembering that.

Love,

Eliza✱Beth

Dear Eliza*Beth,

What an embarrassing memory. . . . Remember how we found out later that the Easter Bunny was actually that weird science teacher, Mr. Copeland? (I think he was probably moonlighting . . . bunny lighting . . . to earn money to buy a new toupee.) I can't believe I used to do such dumb things. (It was fun, though!!!!)

What an awful conversation with your mom. You wrote it so that I actually felt like I was there with both of you. (The things your mom told you made me feel so uncomfortable, so terrible.) I can't believe that you're standing up for yourself so much. You're being soooo brave. I am sooooooooooooooooooooo proud of you.

I'm also so angry at your parents . . . yes, your parentS. Obviously, I'm furious at your dad. He's being more immature than my parents ever were, and you know how bad that was sometimes. But I'm also mad at your mother. (Even though I think she was really great to talk to you and let you know the truth.) I just don't know how your mother let this happen. Doesn't she talk to your father? I know you can't talk to him, but she's a GROWN-UP.

Eliza*Beth . . . don't get mad at me for saying this. You're always so nice . . . and you always try to see the best in everyone . . . but I know that you're really depressed and scared and unhappy . . . and you didn't do anything to cause it . . . and you don't deserve what's happening. It's so upsetting. If you won't get angry at your parents then I will!!!!!!!!!!!! (But I'm not as angry at your mom as at your dad.)

About my life . . . it's a shambles!!!! We've had so much snow here, the play has been postponed three times. (We kept having postponement parties instead of cast parties.) And then everyone got the flu and a lot of the cast got sick. If we had put the play on then, instead of calling it *Cheaper by the Dozen*, we would have had to call it *Cheaper by the Half Dozen*.

Oh, guess what????????? My heart is broken. (Well, at least it's dented.) Old what's-his-face, Alex, doesn't want to go out with me anymore. He says that he wants to wait until eighth grade to date. I tell you. Seventh-grade boys can be soooooo immature. Oh, well . . . Barb thinks it's for the best, that I'm "too young" and that now I'll be able to devote myself to my studies and go out when I'm much older. (Think about it. . . . My mom was married at seventeen and had me before she was eighteen and she's talking about "too young.") Anyway, dating in seventh grade is not very serious. We just say we're going out, and we get a few Chee-to kisses and talk on the phone. (Actually, I did most of the talking.) You know, Eliza*Beth, I really miss being able to talk to you on the phone at least a gazillion times a day. . . .

Other news. . . . I'm thinking of having one of my ears double pierced and the other triple pierced. Remember when you went with me when I got them single pierced? That was sooo fun. (Do you think your parents will ever let you get yours single pierced? Maybe you should try to get them done now, while your parents aren't paying as much attention to you. Hannah's going to get her ears double pierced too. We'll go together. This time I promise not to pretend to faint. (You were so embarrassed when I did that!!!)

Anyway . . . I hope things get better for you.

Gotta go.

As always,

Tara Starr

Elizabeth

Dear Tara*Starr,

My mother is doing her best. Can't you see that? Give her a little credit. You know, sometimes you are very hard on people. You get these ideas about how things should be, what's right, what's wrong, what is, what isn't, and you won't let go of them. I want to tell you just to let things be, but I know we can't control people's reactions. Mrs. Jackson said that. She's not a therapist or anything. She just says cool things. (I've been talking to her again.) But she's right. We can't control how people react to things we do or say.

How they react is in *their* control. So I'm not going to tell you to let things be, even though I wish you would. But I can tell you to consider where my mother is coming from. Maybe Barb wouldn't have done what my mother has done all these years, but Barb and Mom are two different people. How do we know what being married to my father is like? I think my mom has wanted to have a job for a long time now. I mean, doesn't staying at home all day sound *boring*? But who knows what my dad has said when Mom told him she wanted to go to work. He might have threatened her or something. It isn't like my mom is *lazy*. I think she's been scared. And I am really REALLY proud of her for taking charge of things now, even if *you* think she should have done that a long time ago.

I'm not mad at you, Tara. But I wish you would look at things through other people's eyes instead of just your own. About my father — I'm furious at him too. But I'm not sure that what he's doing is immature. I mean, it *is* immature, but I think something *else* is going on. I think he has a problem. Like a psychological problem. I'm not sure.

Those credit people are really after us. They not

only send letters (and a lot more come now than before), but they call all the time (we're not allowed to answer the phone anymore, the answering machine does that), *and* a couple of times they have come to the door. Luckily, Mom figured out who they were and told us to hide instead of answering the bell. But get this. Dad is still charging stuff on credit cards (using ones he hasn't gotten in trouble with yet). He does this partly because it's the only way we can buy things, and partly because *I really think he has a problem*. He bought Emma a *playhouse* last week. It arrived yesterday. Mom couldn't help herself — she gave Dad a look that plainly said, "What is *wrong* with you?" And I thought my father was going to cry. He just said "I'm sorry" and walked away.

Here's the good thing. Mom stood up very straight, marched to the phone, called the toy store, and asked for someone to come pick up the playhouse. She said it was a mistake. She said we couldn't afford it. And I never heard a peep about it from Dad. He's very quiet these days. Mom is on the phone a lot. She's up to something (taking charge, Tara), and I'm going to find out what as soon as we have another private talk.

I'm so sorry about your life being a shambles. It better turn around soon. Your life is the only good one I have. I've been waiting and waiting to hear about opening night, and all I hear about are postponement parties. Just kidding. But really, it is frustrating. So when *is* opening night? (I wish I could see the play then.)

And about Alex — what a jerk! But when I think about the boys in some of *my* classes . . . Well, I definitely would not want a spitty Chee-to kiss from any of them. They are so dorky. They carry slime around with them. Also, they think it's the funniest thing in the world if somebody falls over backward in his (or her) chair. Please. Grow up. Get a life. Right?

Love,

Eliza ✱ *Beth*

P.S. Did you and Hannah get your ears pierced? I can't wait to find out.

P.P.S. I don't think I want my ears pierced yet. I probably *could* get them done now. But I think I might wait until I'm older.

February 10

Dear Eliza*Beth

Sometimes I just don't know what to do, what to say, when I get your letters and answer them!!!!!!!!

Here goes:

I have only one set of eyes, <u>MINE</u> — and sometimes I see things that YOU don't want to see. . . . YOU ARE MY BEST FRIEND!!!!!! Am I supposed to just see things that are really major, really important, and not say anything??????????

And I know that things are *bad* for you, so:

1. I *try* not to be so extreme in what I say to you.

2. I try not to show you what I truly feel — how really happy I am sometimes, how sad I get over some things in my life. (The things that bother me seem soooooo small. My major shambles is that a Chee-to kisser broke up with me. Your shambles is that you are hiding behind sofas from creditors and not answering the phone. I could NEVER not answer a phone!!!)

I do get angry at you sometimes. I want you to yell, to be stronger, to march up to your father and tell him "STOP IT." (I do know that you've been trying . . . but I want you to do something major, to say the magic thing that will make everything all better.)

Oh, Eliza*Beth. . . . I've just reread what I've written and realize that there is no magic solution AND I can see that you and your mom are trying, are changing — that you are both standing up for yourselves much more. It just feels like baby steps when

138

what you need to do is to "take a really strong stand" to stop your father from doing what he's doing.

Look, Eliza*Beth — I know that I don't see things out of other people's eyes. It's sometimes hard enough seeing things clearly in my own life. (So . . . sometimes I'm a little nearsighted, and I'm not talking medically.) But you know that I care — and you also know that I'm right a lot of the time. Well, most of the time.

So, I really do think you should understand that I only say things to help you because I care. (And I really do think you and your mom should be doing a lot more.)

Okay, . . . now for the news you asked me to tell you.

The play <u>finally</u> went on. . . . I remembered all my lines. (However, when I looked at the video that Luke took, I saw that my bra strap showed for the whole first act. I am sooooo embarrassed!!!!!!) And then one of my "brothers" tripped over his shoelace and gave himself a nosebleed. (His shirt looked really awful and he didn't have a change of clothes, so for the second act he wore a Brady Bunch sweatshirt.) Also, the dog peed on the stage . . . and Alex slipped on it. (Tsk. Tsk.)

The cast party was lots of fun — music, dancing (a little Chee-to throwing too). No slime, though, not unless you count Alvin "the Nerd" Henderson, who likes to "floss his nose" and who tells girls that he'd be glad to floss their noses. (It was funny, though, when he offered to floss Danielle Banford's nose, since she is a very snotty person.)

I just got my ears pierced. (Again.) Hannah got hers done too. She's mad at me, though, because I keep calling her Elizabeth.

Love,

Tara Starr

Elizabeth

To Tara:

This was going to be a Valentine's Day greeting, but not after reading your last letter. Tara, I do not understand you anymore. What is wrong with you? Do you *ever* listen to yourself? Do you ever listen to *me*? Are you incapable of sympathy, even sympathy for the person you call a friend? Look up "sympathy" in the dictionary. One of the definitions is "the ability to enter into another person's mental state, feelings, emotions, etc." Why can't you do that anymore? I'm trying to remember if you've always been unsympathetic and judgmental and I just didn't notice, or if this is something new.

Tara, you truly are not hearing what I'm telling you and when occasionally you do hear some little something, you decide it's not good enough for you. What do I have to do? Fly to Ohio, take you by the shoulders, and shake you?

LISTEN.

I am telling you that my mom and I *are* doing things. In my last letter, I told you she even admitted to whoever answered the phone at the store that we couldn't afford the playhouse. I told you that she's planning something (I just don't know what). The point is that Mom *is* taking charge. But you can't stand that she isn't doing it your way. I think you have a problem with control, Tara.

And speaking of problems, I wrote to you that my father has problems. Something is wrong with him. He's sick in some way. SICK, Tara. So can't you feel some sympathy for him even though he's done a lot of wrong, bad things?

You know what? I don't think I can write to you anymore. I don't need to spend so much of my time defending myself. I need my energy for all the *changes* my mother and I are making. Plus, you no longer feel like a friend to me, Tara.

So this is it.

Goodbye.

Elizabeth

P.S. I never said we hide behind couches when the doorbell rings. I just said we hide. But you make stuff up, Tara, and then you try to build a case on it — and yell at me for something you made up.

Enjoy your life, Tara.

February 18

ELIZABETH —

Good-bye forever.

How dare you write to me like that?

Excuse me for trying to be the best friend that I know how to be.

Obviously that's not good enough for you — so, again, GOOD-BYE FOREVER . . .

. . . but before I go, I've got a few things to say.

1. So you're not hiding behind couches — but you did say you were "hiding." . . . You

said that, didn't you? So I imagined that it was behind couches. You've always said that "my active imagination" was something you liked.

2. Your father is "sick." Oh, Elizabeth . . . You can look at it any way you want — and I'll even admit that you're probably right — but you know, although we never talk about it, that I don't like him. He's never been nice to me. The only reason he let us be friends is because you and your mom made him be polite to me. He's always been so "snobby." If you have to call someone "judgmental," maybe it should be *him*.

3. I don't need you as a friend. I have lots of friends here . . . and I had (and have) lots of friends there. But don't worry, I won't discuss any of your problems with them. (And I never have. I was a better friend than you know. I've always supported you — when everyone talked about how shy and quiet you are, and some people even thought you were "snobby" because you hardly ever talk to

anyone — I always told them how nice and smart and funny and fun and kind you are. I guess I won't be saying that anymore.) I won't be nasty and end this letter like you did with "Enjoy your life" . . . but by saying "Thank you very much. I *will* enjoy my life."

Tara Starr

February 25

Eliza*Beth —
Please write back. I'm worried about you.

Tara*Starr

March 4

ELIZA*BETH

I really am worried about you.

Also, I miss you.

I know that I said I have lots of friends . . . but there is no one like you. Things happen here and I want to tell you or write to you about them. No one understands me the way you do. (And I bet no one understands you the way I do.)

I've been doing a lot of thinking. Maybe I am a little judgmental — and maybe I don't always listen the way I should . . . but you don't always say things out loud, so I try to fill in the gaps. And Barb does say that I've got a lot of growing up to do. She also says that I shouldn't be so hard on myself for not being perfect, that no one is perfect. So I'm sorry that you're so angry at me, but *neither* of us is perfect.

I really wish that you would write back — or answer the messages I've left for you on your answering machine.

Tara Starr

Okay. THIS IS IT.

If you don't want to be my friend — okay.

But do me a favor. Please fill out this card. (Send it to Barb if you won't send it to me.)

☐ I am alive and okay and so is my family.

☐ My life is terrible but leave me alone. I'm alive.

☐ I'm talking to someone who can help me.

☐ I know that you, Tara*Starr, are sorry and I forgive you.

☐ I, Eliza*Beth, am sorry too and I miss you.

Good-bye.

*Tara*Starr*

March 17

⊠ I am alive and okay and so is my family.

☐ My life is terrible but leave me alone. I'm alive.

⊠ I'm talking to someone who can help me.

⊠ I know that you, Tara*Starr, are sorry and I forgive you.

⊠ I, Eliza*Beth, am sorry too and I miss you.

152

Dear Tara*Starr,

I was just going to send this postcard back all by itself, but I need to ask you one very important question. Do you still want to be friends? I think you do, but I have to make sure. *I* still want to be friends. Also, I have a LOT to tell you.

Love,

Elizabeth

March 22

ELIZABETH

YES! YES!!! YES!!!!!!!!!!!!!!!!!!!!!!!!!!!!!!!!!!!!!!! Of course I still want to be friends.

TELL ME WHAT'S GOING ON!!!!!!!!!!!!!!!!!

Love,

Tara Starr

March 28

Dear Tara*Starr,

I've been thinking for a long time about what to say in this letter. And I feel I have to start by being FRANK and HONEST and telling you what I am really thinking, without holding anything back. I am thinking that I am sorry we had a letter-fight, but I am not sorry about any of the things I said because I meant them all. (This is just me, saying things out loud, even if they're on paper.) I *am* sorry, though, for telling you to have a nice life. That was kind of mean, and I know it.

155

You admitted that you can be judgmental and that you're not perfect. So I'll admit that I don't always say things out loud. That's true. What's also true is that I'm changing. And I'm saying way more things than I used to say. I just wish you could see that, instead of thinking I'm not changing. It feels a little like you don't *want* me to change, and so you see me the way I used to be. (And you see my mother the way she used to be.) Is that true? Or maybe it's just really hard being friends on paper. I think our friendship would be different if we could still see each other every day.

Anyway, I'm sorry we had a fight, and I do miss you and I love you and I'm glad you want to be my friend. I've *really* missed catching you up on all my news. I do tell my news to Mrs. Jackson, though. I talk to her all the time now. And I'm writing more and more poetry and showing it to her. She says it's very good. I like talking to Mrs. Jackson, but there's nothing like talking to a friend who's your own age. A friend you've known a long time. A friend who knows almost everything about you that there is to know. That's you, Tara.

So . . . here's what's been happening. It's really an

awful lot. I think you'll have a hard time believing me, but every bit of it is true.

First of all, take a good look at the address on the envelope. It's one of the last times you'll see it. We're going to be moving soon. And get this. We're moving to a *one*-bedroom apartment. That one bedroom is for Emma and me, so I guess Mom and Dad are going to sleep in the living room, which, I might add, is the only other room, apart from the kitchen and the bathroom. How are we going to fit sixteen rooms of stuff into our apartment, you might ask? We're not (duh). We're going to sell most of it. On Saturday. Don't I sound calm about everything? Well, the truth is (and I know this seems weird), I feel relieved. VERY relieved. Because this is what we have to do to get ourselves out of our $$ problems. And when you consider that I was afraid we'd be living on the streets, this isn't bad at all. An apartment. With a bedroom and a kitchen.

Emma and I have already decided how we're going to set up our room. We're going to get bunk beds (cheapo ones from Value Town). They're going to go at one end of the room. (Bunk beds save space.) Then all of Emma's stuff will go on one side of the room, and all of mine will go on the other. We can each decorate our own wall however we want. That's our deal. Even if Emma wants to put up that hideous clown poster.

Anyway, I'm *way* off track. I have to back up to the middle of February. That was when Mom came into my room one night for a talk. I was already in bed, but I hadn't turned the light out yet. She sat on the edge of the bed and just started talking about all this financial stuff. She said she'd been to see an accountant and a lawyer. Dad had gotten us in Really Big Trouble. (Did you notice that *he* got us into it, but *Mom* is getting us out of it? She's doing this all on her own. Dad just sits around now, watching that home shopping show — but he can't order anything because he doesn't have any more credit cards.) The accountant and the lawyer both told Mom that the only way to save ourselves is to sell our house and almost everything in it, and use the money to pay off our debts. Well, most of them. (I think Mom's parents are going to help pay off what isn't covered.) Then we can pretty much start over.

Okay, Tara, now hold on to your sequined hat. Guess how we're going to pay the rent on our apartment. *Mom got a job.* A *paying* one. At Kate's Kitchen. Isn't that great? Their Director of Development (whatever that is) left, so Kate (she's the head of it all, like you couldn't guess) hired Mom to replace her. Mom has already started, even though we haven't sold the house. Well, technically we have. It's just that it isn't final, plus our apartment isn't vacant yet, so we're still in our house. (Jeannemarie and Martha are gone, though. Mom asked them to leave the very afternoon she came back from seeing the accountant. Martha cried when she left, and Jeannemarie told me to call her anytime, which I might do.)

The way we sold the house so fast is this: Do you remember that day two summers ago when we were sitting in my front yard, painting each other's nails, and a car pulled up and a woman got out? She asked if my parents were home, and when Mom came outside the woman told her we had the most beautiful house she'd ever seen. Then she gave Mom her card and said if we ever decided to sell the house to call her first.

Do you remember? You and I were laughing. We thought this was *so* weird. Like driving up to someone and saying, "You have an incredibly handsome husband. Let me know if you ever get tired of him." I don't know how weird Mom thought it was, but she saved the woman's card and, well, guess who's buying our house. That woman and her husband. The Franklins. They were thrilled. They didn't even question the price. They're going to give Mom what she asked for, as soon as the papers are signed. This should be any day now. Then, like I said, the big sale will take place on Saturday. The Saturday after that, we're supposed to move into the apartment. I guess my next letter will be about the sale.

That's the news. Well, actually, it's just sort of an outline of the news. The main Roman numeral parts. I could fill in lots more details in the smaller categories under the Roman numerals, but I'd wind up writing, like, a whole book. So I'll stop here.

PLEASE, PLEASE, PLEASE write really soon, Tara. I can't wait to hear from you.

What are the things that are happening that you want to tell me about? Do you have any more pierced body parts? How are Barb and Luke? Is Barb p _ _ _ _ _ _ _ yet? (I know I promised I wouldn't ask again, but I didn't *really* ask, since I left out most of the word.)

I miss you.

Love,

Elizabeth

P.S. You'll see that I've taken the * out of my name. No offense, Tara, really. It's just that the * never felt like *me*.

P.P.S. PLEASE let me know what's happening with you. I keep asking, and you keep saying you can't tell me all the good stuff, that you have to hold back, but I am *asking* you to tell me! So tell!!!

March 31

Dear Elizabeth,

　Wow!!!!!!

　Your news is overwhelming.

　I can hardly believe that you are being so calm. (Although I guess you have no choice.)

　I have to answer your letter with a list. That's the only way I can be organized.

　1. I don't want to get into another fight but I do want to defend myself. I DO KNOW THAT YOU'RE CHANGING. . . . I've always

wanted you to be able to say what you feel, do what you want. (Even if I don't agree all the time.) I do hate that you have changed so much, have had to be soooooo grown-up, so serious . . . I mean we're just kids. (I always thought that I had to be the grown-up in my family until now, but it was more fun. Your problems are so serious.) Anyway, I am very proud of you . . . and I do think your mom is doing amazing things . . . getting the new job, selling the house and the things in it. I CAN SEE THAT YOU ARE CHANGING. The only thing I'm worried about is . . . are you always going to get mad when I don't agree with you, when I don't see things the way you do? (That sounds like what you accused me of doing.) It is sooooo hard writing letters and not seeing each other. It makes our friendship hard work sometimes. It used to be so much easier when we saw each other all the time. Now, in some ways, it's so different. But I want us to be friends forever. Can't you just see us as little old ladies sitting in our rocking chairs, knitting and talking? (Actually you'll probably be knitting and I'll be sewing sequins and beads on everything.)

2. It's great that you have Mrs. Jackson to talk to about what's happening. It used to make me really nervous when I thought I was the only person that you could talk to. That's one of the reasons I kept trying to give you advice.

3. I'm sorry you have to move into such a small place. I remember when Luke and Barb and I had to live in a one-bedroom apartment. (I was the one who had to sleep in the living room . . . which was probably, in my family, best, because I think that Luke and Barb need a lot of privacy.) I can't imagine how it's going to work out for you but I hope it will be okay. (Maybe you can turn the clown poster into a dart board.) It's going to be weird writing to you and not knowing what the place where you're opening the letter looks like. What are you going to be able to keep and take to the new place? Are you going to be able to keep your television set?

(So that your father can still watch the Home Shopping Network . . . Oh, Elizabeth, I know that was mean . . . but you can't expect me to change totally . . . not about your father, at least.)

Now, about the questions about me and my family . . . I have no more pierced body parts (none planned either). I did paint my fingernails magenta and paste tiny rhine-stones on them. As for Barb and the "p-word," I DON'T THINK SO!!!!!! Barb's got the flu this week . . . so the only "p-words" for her are "puke, projectile vomiting, and pretty tired." She thinks she caught the flu from Luke, who had it last week and who had the same symptoms. I only hope that I don't catch it, because I have a DATE next week. . . . I'm going out with a NINTH-grader. Vinnie. He's sooooo cute . . . and smart . . . and he doesn't eat Chee-tos!!!!! Luke thinks that Vin-nie's too old for me. (Luke's getting a little weird about my growing up. He's making a lot more rules than he used to.)

Anyway, I am so very absolutely positively glad that we're friends again.

Love,

Tara✷Starr

(I'm keeping the star in my name because I still love it, but I don't mind that you've changed your name back again. In my brain, I always kept calling you Elizabeth. . . . You were the one who wanted to try out a new name. . . . Well, I guess we'll both be trying out new stuff while we're growing up, and I guess that not all of it is going to work.) Again, much love.

P.S. I will try not to hold back. . . . I will "tell" what's going on in my life even though I don't know if it's right to feel so good when things are so bad for you. Here goes:

1. I have friends from all the different groups and I'm going to lots of parties.

2. Luke and Barb gave me my own telephone and my own number — and I get lots of calls. The only bad part is that I have to wash the dishes to "pay" for the phone.

3. Two weeks ago I joined the school newspaper and already the advisor called me "a rising star" (a rising starr, she should say).

April 5

Dear Tara*Starr,

I received your letter two days ago, but every time I sit down to answer it I get interrupted. I really wanted to answer you *right away,* because I am just so glad that our fight is over and we're friends again, even if we have to settle for being letter-friends. Anyway, I finally have time to write.

Tara, I was *expecting* you to keep the star in your name (especially since you are now a rising star). I didn't think you'd drop it just because I dropped mine. And I know I was the one who asked for a new

168

name. I'm not accusing you of trying to force it on me or something. I just looked around and decided I'm more of an Elizabeth than an Eliza*Beth. And I *like* being Elizabeth. That's all I meant.

How is Barb feeling? Better, I hope. That is a disgusting bug. Emma had it last month. It was going around Miss Fine's, but luckily none of us caught it from Emma.

Well, guess what. We sold our stuff on Saturday. Most of it, anyway. Get this. An *auctioneer* came over with some people from the bank and they auctioned everything right in our yard. Have you ever heard of such a thing? That auctioneer made a lot of money. The bank people seemed pleased. (And no wonder, since all the $$ went directly to the bank to help pay off what we owe.) Anyway, I don't know how the auction was advertised but, like, a million people showed up for it. (Well, about 200.) And you should have seen people bidding on things. When they *really* wanted something they would just keep topping each other. This one woman bought an antique desk for seven *thousand* dollars. And the bidding had started at $1,500.

Anyway, here's what we get to keep and take to our new apt.:

Emma's dresser	sofa bed
my dresser	Mom and Dad's dressers
my desk	armchair
my bookcase	TV
a lot of Emma's toys	coffee table
our clothes	kitchen table and chairs
all my personal stuff	stereo
(books, projects, etc.)	small items like clocks
my sewing machine	kitchen things
Emma's clown poster	

See? It isn't *so* bad. Just, well, less. Less of everything. Less stuff, less space. And as far as I'm concerned, less to worry about. Tara, you said I don't have any choice but to be calm. But didn't you hear me in my last letter? I said I was RELIEVED. And when I say something, I mean it. I know my family's problems are *far* from over. But we're getting back on our feet, Tara. We're getting out of debt. We won't have people sending us threatening letters or, worse, coming to our door demanding we return things that

Dad hasn't paid for. I think we need to have less. Now we'll live in a small apartment that won't cost much to rent, and Mom will have her job at Kate's Kitchen. It isn't going to pay us *quite* enough at first, but my grandparents said they can make up the difference every month for one year. And Mom has been PROMISED a promotion with a raise in November, which is only seven months away. (Kate wanted to give her the higher salary now, but she's waiting for grant $$ to come through, whatever that means.)

Guess what. I was in Mrs. Jackson's office yesterday and the COOLEST thing happened. She told me she's thinking of letting the students start a poetry journal that could be published in our school newspaper office. It could come out three or four times a year. She would be the advisor, and — if she really gets the project going — she wants me to be the *editor*. Isn't that excellent? *Me*. The editor of a poetry journal. She wants to start it right away so we could get one issue out by the end of the year. Then we could start again in the fall (EIGHTH GRADE!!!) and I would be the editor all year. I am so excited I can hardly stand it.

Guess what else. Moving day is in TWO (2) days.

Part of me can't believe it and is nervous. The other part of me can't wait. We've been living in our huge house with almost no furniture for five days now, and it's like living in a mausoleum. Some of the rooms are entirely empty and they actually echo. I'll be glad to get out of here. For some reason, I keep thinking of that movie *The Shining* — with the enormous haunted hotel and the crazy father. The Franklins are going to move into our house next weekend.

So . . . HOW WAS YOUR DATE WITH VINNIE? Did he kiss you? What did you wear? Where did you go? I can't wait to hear.

Oh, I almost forgot — save the envelope this letter came in. I put my new address on it. Do you recognize it? Our apartment is in that complex kind of near the shopping center.

WRITE BACK SOON (please).

Love,

Elizabeth

P.S. Say hi to Barb and Luke for me.

P.P.S. What do your fingernails look like now?

Dear Elizabeth,

Wow. There sure is a lot happening with you.

I'm glad you are relieved with the way things are going. I know that I could never handle things the way you do. I know that I could never have been there if all our stuff was auctioned off. (Did you know any of the people who came to the auction? Was the desk that was sold for $7000.00 the one I once accidentally spilled soda on that time your Dad yelled at me . . . actually one of the times your Dad yelled at me. And how is he doing? Is he feeling any better?) I hope you don't mind that I'm asking questions and making comments about the auction.

Is the apartment building that you are moving to the one Susie Maldrey lives in? I think so. She had a pajama party there once and it looked like a nice place. Maybe now that you'll be living there, you two can get to know each other. She's really nice and she likes to read and write too. Maybe she'll be on the staff of your poetry journal. By the way, congratulations. That's such great news!!!!!!!! Oh, I'm going to be doing a humor column for my school newspaper. It's going to be called Tara*Starr Signs (sort of like an astrologer making predictions, but really it's just going to be a way for me to comment on the world as I see it . . . and you know how much I love doing that).

My date with Vinnie was a dud. He spent the entire time at the movie squeezing a pimple on his face and then he wanted to hold my hand with the hand that had squeezed, popped, and wiped off the pimple goop. It was so disgusting. I wanted to puke.

And speaking of puking, I'm going to tell you

something but I don't ever want to discuss it or have it mentioned again. Barbara is pregnant. It wasn't the flu after all.

As for my fingernails, I've bitten them all off.

Love,

Tara Starr

Elizabeth

Dear Tara*Starr,

My father is gone. He left us. I wanted to write
and tell you sooner — the day it happened — but I
just couldn't. I still can't believe it. None of us can.
Mom is in shock. And Emma is being the most incredible spoiled pill of a child. (Mom says she's acting
out.) I'm in shock too, I guess. But do you know
what? This is a HUGE secret, but one teeny little part
of me is RELIEVED. Just like when we sold the house.
But only a *teeny* part of me. The rest is, well, I'm not
sure what.

The way it happened was that on Saturday, which was moving day, Dad simply didn't go with us to the apartment. A van had arrived at our house early in the morning. Two movers had loaded up the furniture and boxes and now the van was on its way across town to the apartment complex. Mom and Dad and I had put the little things that weren't going in the van into the back of the station wagon. (Did I tell you we sold our other cars at the auction?) I had strapped Emma in her seat and climbed in next to her. Mom was standing by the passenger door at the front of the car. We were waiting for Dad to come out of the house and drive us to the apartment. Instead he stood on the porch and called Mom to him. And at that moment a taxi pulled up, which was really weird. Mom and Dad stood on the front porch and talked quietly — for just a few minutes. Then they walked to the car. Dad was in front and Mom was behind him and they both looked so sad. Just . . . sad.

Dad leaned into the backseat of the car and said, "Girls, I have something to tell you. I'm not coming with you today. I need a little space, some time to myself. I have to figure some things out. So . . . you go to the new place, you and your mom. I'll be in touch next week." Then he kissed us both, got in the taxi, and left.

Just like that.

Mom and Emma and I were absolutely silent on the drive to the apartment. Then Mom pulled into the parking lot, found our space (#28), switched off the ignition, and just sat for a moment. When she turned around, she wasn't crying or anything, but she looked like a different person. (I can't really explain what I mean.)

"Elizabeth, Emma," she said, "I did not know this was going to happen."

Tara, you probably don't believe that, but I do. You just have to have seen my mom. And heard her. It was like someone had said, "Ma'am, it turns out that the world is flat after all." Like she'd learned that something she had counted on and taken for granted had turned out not to be true, and she had never suspected a thing.

"He didn't say anything to you?" I asked.

"Not a word. And everything he owns, except for what he's wearing, is in the moving van."

"So he *is* coming back," I said.

Before Mom could answer, Emma said, "When? When is he coming back?"

"I don't know," Mom replied.

Well, guess what. Dad has been gone for a week and he hasn't called. We don't even know where he went. How much "space" does he need? He said he would be in touch "next week." To me, that meant sometime between Monday and Friday. And here it is, Saturday.

For the first two or three days Mom concentrated on unpacking. She decided not to do anything about Dad. But by Tuesday night she was worried. She called his brother and his parents. They don't know where he is. On Wednesday she called some of the people he used to work with. No one has heard from him.

We're okay money-wise, Tara. Mom got this apartment without any help from Dad. Her parents cosigned the lease, and like I explained, we can live on her salary with help from Nana and Grandpa until she gets her raise in November. So we're really all right for all the basic stuff — the apartment, food, clothes. (In some ways we're better off than we were over the winter.) But WHERE IS MY FATHER? I know you hate him, Tara, and don't care what happens to

him. However, he *is* my father. He's part of my life. I
don't know if I miss him, exactly. (I certainly don't
miss the person he had become), but I'm worried
about him. So is Mom. And Emma does miss him.
Also, she's confused about the move, and all the
changes. Now she goes to day care after Miss Fine's
ends. She still goes to Miss Fine's, because Dad paid
for the full year back in August. She is a miserable,
crabby pill. This morning she was so rotten that I had
to leave the apartment to get away from her. Here's
the good thing about our apartment: It is just two
blocks from the public library, so that's where I went.
I wrote some poems.

This is one:

> The days fall away like petals
> Coming to rest at my feet.
> The hours tick along.
> People pass on the street.
>
> The days fall away like petals.
> My father is gone.

It doesn't have a title yet. Can you think of one?

I have so much more to tell you, Tara. I want to tell you about the apartment and our first week here, about who else lives in the complex. (By the way, I found out that the complex has a name. DEER RUN. Isn't that ridiculous? If anyone EVER sees a deer here I will pay him $1,000. I'm going to put all that stuff in my next letter, though.

Just one more thing. I know you said never to mention that Barb is pregnant, but how can I not mention it? I mean, not mentioning a baby at your house is like not commenting on an elephant in the living room. (That's something Dad used to say. The part about the elephant, I mean.) Tara, I think it's wonderful news and I'm very happy for Barb and Luke. I hope I get to see the baby one day. I couldn't stand never knowing your little sister or brother. I know that you aren't happy, though, so I won't say anything more right now. Just please tell Barb and Luke congratulations from me.

Lots of love,

Elizabeth

April 20

Dear Elizabeth,

I'm sorry. I'm really sorry. I don't know what else to say. It all sounds so awful. I feel so bad for you and your mom and Emma.

I'm not going to say anything about your father because he is your father and I know that you care about him and are worried about him.

About your poem . . . maybe you should call it "He loves us. He loves us not." Remember when we used to do that with flowers when we liked some boy . . . and you do talk about petals falling off.

Elizabeth . . . I really believe that your mom didn't know what your father was going to do. Please don't keep saying that I'm not going to believe something before I don't believe it. You talk about how you and your mom are changing. I can change too. And in this case, I don't doubt what you're saying . . . okay . . . I guess I do doubt a lot about your father . . . but I'm learning not to say anything about it to you.

I'm sorry that Emma is so unhappy and is being "a miserable, crabby pill." It's a good thing the library is close to your house so that you can escape from your sister and the apartment for a while. (We also live near a library. That's going to come in handy for me in the future too.)

I hope things get better for you soon.

As for congratulating Barbara and Lucas, you have their address. Send them a note. At the moment, we're not speaking.

Love,

Tara Starr

Elizabeth

April 26

Dear Tara*Starr,

I promise I won't say another word about the b _ _ _ — after this paragraph. I just have to say these few things here and then I won't mention the subject again until *you* bring it up. I'm enclosing a note for Barb and Luke. I know you said I have their address, which I assumed meant that I was supposed to mail a note to them separately, but I'm trying to save the cost of a postage stamp. (I'm doing some baby-sitting here at DEER RUN, so I'm earning my own $$, but I'm being as thrifty as possible. I just have to be. There is

185

not one spare cent for anything extra.) Anyway, I put your parents' note in its own envelope and sealed it so you don't even have to look at the letter. And you won't have to say anything about it to your parents. The envelope speaks for itself. It says TO BARB AND LUKE FROM ELIZABETH on the outside. See? Just leave it on the kitchen table or someplace. Okay? Thank you. That is my last word about the b _ _ _.

Well, we've been here at DEER RUN for almost three weeks. Here are some of the pros and cons about it:

PROS	CONS
We can afford it.	It isn't very attractive.
I like having other people around.	Sometimes I feel like I'm living in a fish-bowl.
Two blocks from library	Across the street from a row of gas stations
Four blocks from Dunkin' Donuts	Four blocks from Fred's Fish Fry
Six blocks from Chuck E. Cheez (Emma's pro)	Six blocks from Chuck E. Cheez (my con)

Nine kids from our school live here. We live on the first floor, so we have a little garden. One of them is Karen Frank's best friend. Mom worries about our safety.

We're pretty much unpacked now. We're crowded, but it isn't too bad.

Oh, Tara. We still haven't heard from my father. No one has. Mom wants to file a missing person's report with the police, but the thing is, Dad left voluntarily. I mean, he *told* us he needed to be alone for a while. It isn't as if he called from the office and said, "I'll be home in fifteen minutes," and then never showed up and his car was located in a parking lot, with blood everywhere. He said he was leaving and he left. He just hasn't been in touch like he said he would be. So we're waiting, but I'm not sure for what. A phone call? A letter? Until my uncle says, "Okay, *now* we should go to the police"? Until three years pass and Mom meets someone nice and wants to marry him, but she can't because she isn't divorced from Dad, so she *has* to do something about finding him?

I'm mad at my father for putting Mom in this position when she has so many other things to do right now. Like she needs *this* too? She's trying to juggle her new job, Emma's day care, our new apartment, a whole new life — and do it all by herself. I know that lots of single moms do this, but my mother at least needs a little time to get used to it. I think things will be better when we get to know more people at DEER RUN, and Mom can share carpooling with other parents or whatever. Right now, for instance, she spends her lunch hour dashing across town to pick up Emma at Miss Fine's and drive her to the day care center for the afternoon. Then Mom spends the weekends cleaning and running errands. (She decided to devote evenings to Emma and me, even though it's nobody's best time. Mom and Emma come home at 6:00 every night, exhausted, but we do have those few hours together.)

I help out, of course. I get home first every day, and I'm in charge of grocery shopping and making dinner. I'm learning to cook, Tara! Guess what. It's kind of fun. I like it. Mom likes that I do these things, but she doesn't demand it. And she knows that starting next week I won't get home until 5:00 on Tuesdays and Thursdays. She says we'll just keep things in the freezer — casseroles and stews — that we can thaw out in the microwave for quick suppers those nights.

Why won't I get home until 5:00? Because I will have poetry journal meetings on those afternoons. The poetry journal really is going to happen, and I really am going to be the student editor!!!! I CANNOT WAIT!!!! I will tell you about it in my next letter.

Write soon, okay?

Love,

Elizabeth

April 26

Dear Barb and Luke,

CONGRATULATIONS!! Tara told me about the baby (but as you know she doesn't want to talk about it, so I have to write b _ _ _ in *her* letters). But *I* think the news is great. Isn't it wonderful to have something like that to look forward to? A *baby*! A brand-new BABY! Are you thinking of names yet? I kind of hope the baby is another girl. You could name her Mary. It's plain, but it's one of my favorites. Or what about Emily, Allison, Paige, Grace, or Anna? Of course, a boy would be fine too. Michael is a nice name.

Anyway, congratulations! I hope I get to see the baby one day.

Love,

Elizabeth

P.S. I guess Tara has told you all my news. Except for not knowing about my father, things are pretty much better now.

April 30

Dear Elizabeth,

I was just looking at the date on this letter.

It's the end of April.

Who would have thought that so much would be happening when we started writing to each other at the beginning of the school year? (I don't know if I've mentioned it, but I'm three inches taller . . . two shoe sizes bigger . . . and my bra size is bigger too. . . . Now I actually have a reason to wear a bra. And that's just the physical stuff!!!!!!!!!!!)

When I looked at the date, I thought about that song — you know, April showers bring May flowers. I know that probably sounds "goopy," but maybe it's true. Now you're editor of the poetry journal and two blocks from the library (remember how we used to go there every weekend and pick out our weekly books?) and four blocks from Dunkin' Donuts. (Yum. Remember how we used to go there after the library? . . . You used to get the whole-wheat ones and I used to get the ones filled with custard and covered with vanilla icing and multicolored sprinkles. . . . I really miss doing that.)

About the "con" stuff in your letter. . . . I'm sorry that the place isn't very attractive. . . . It scares me that your mom is worried about your safety. (Please don't think I'm overdramatic for saying that.) As for being six blocks from Chuck E. Cheez . . . I'm with Emma on that one. That would definitely be one of my "pros." (Please say hello to Emma for me. Tell her I miss her and that if I still lived there I would love to go the "The Chuckster's" with her and jump up and down in that little cage with all the balls.)

I'm really sorry that you haven't heard from your father.

I think it's great that you're learning to cook. If you want, I can send you some of the recipes I've used. . . . Remember the marshmallow meat loaf?????!!!!! You probably don't want that recipe!!!

I left your letter to Barbara and Lucas on the table. They probably got it, since it's not there anymore.

Well, that's it for now. Gotta go.

Much love,

Tara Starr

April 30

My dear Elizabeth,

Yes . . . Tara Starr has told us all of your news. (At least she did tell us before she stopped talking to us.) . . . but she left your letter to her on the table with the letter you sent to us. She also left a note saying that we could read it. So, I am aware of all that is happening. You and your mother are being very brave . . . and it sounds like you are being a wonderful helper. That's very important to her, I am sure. She must appreciate it so much and love you so much, although she may be too exhausted to tell you. Honey, you

195

know that you can call us collect anytime. Please do so if you need us.

As for the baby . . . yes. Luke and I are very excited. We very much wanted this baby . . . and have been trying for a while. (I hope that doesn't embarrass you.) We had Tara when we were practically children ourselves. Now that we're twenty-nine we feel much more qualified and ready to be parents than we did when we were seventeen.

Luke and I are trying not to be hard on Tara Starr right now, although she's being impossible. There were a lot of years when we weren't very responsible. We were (I hope) never <u>bad</u> parents. We just never managed to be organized, hold down jobs, save money. Tara Starr was, as soon as she was old enough, the most responsible person in the family . . . keeping things in order, trying to get everything on schedule (planning and making meals), worrying about money. I'm ashamed to admit this, but it took a long time for Luke and me to grow up. Well, now we are (mostly), and it's been hard for Tara Starr to adjust. Just when she was getting used to her parents as grown-ups and herself as "the kid," I got pregnant.

So Tara Starr is angry and confused. Luke and I understand why, and we're sorry that it wasn't easier for her . . . but we have lives too . . . and we want to have this baby.

I hope this helps you to understand why Tara Starr is acting the way she is. Actually, she's acknowledging that there's going to be a baby. As she walked by the other day, she turned to me and snarled, "Why don't you name it 'IT' or 'DemonSeed.'" I really do like your name choices much better, Elizabeth.

Again . . . know that you can call us anytime day or night.

I hope that things get better . . . and that you find out where your father is.

Love,

Barb

P.S. Luke sends his love too.

May 7

Dear Tara*Starr,

I would *love* to have your recipes. Do you really have some? I mean, all written out on cards and everything? I found a kids' cookbook at the library, but most of the "recipes" in it are for, like, celery with peanut butter. I do *not* call this a recipe. Under the Meats section there *are* two casseroles, but I've made each of them four times already. Mom and Emma have been very polite about this, but I know they're thinking enough is enough. (At this point they would probably love your marshmallow meat loaf.)

As for our safety, it scares me too. I never really thought about safety when we lived in our house. We had that fancy alarm system and all the gates and locks. And if you *feel* safe I guess you don't go around *thinking* about how safe you feel. So I didn't think about it here at DEER RUN until I noticed Mom checking and rechecking the locks on our doors and windows (especially the sliding door to the little patio) before we go to bed at night. Everything *has* a lock, but Mom thinks it would be pretty easy for someone to get in our apartment anyway. (She won't even let us sleep with the windows open right now.)

Here is how Mom is going to take care of this: Since Nana and Grandpa said they could help us out every month for a year, but we only need their help until Mom gets a raise in November, Mom is going to ask if they could buy us a simple alarm system with the rest of the money. I'm sure they'll say yes. Then we'll all feel better.

Anyway . . . here is the big news. The poetry journal is underway. Mrs. Jackson posted signs about it around school, and six kids besides me have joined. They are Howie Besser, Nancy Jordan, Fiona Hancock, Evan Werner, Sandra Rossner, and (you won't believe this) Susie Maldrey. And yes, Susie does live at DEER RUN. So does Howie. Susie has a little brother who's Emma's age, so Mom might have a car-pooling buddy pretty soon.) After the very first journal meeting Susie and Howie and I walked home together. We walked home together after the second meeting, too, and then we started walking to and from school every day! Susie is really nice. So is Howie. Howie's mother died last year, so he and his father are on their own. His father owns one of the gas stations across the street. Susie's mother has a desktop publishing business in their living room, and her father works at the library. (Isn't that cool? Imagine working at the *library*.)

Anyway, everyone on my staff (Mrs. Jackson lets me call the other kids "my staff," even though technically we are all *her* staff) has been assigned a job and we've come up with a title for the journal. It's *Silhouette*. Like that poem by Langston Hughes? A very disturbing poem, but it's Nancy's favorite, and Langston Hughes is currently my favorite poet (do you know "Mother to Son"?), so we all voted for *Silhouette*. We will put out one edition at the end of the year and then get back to work in the fall. Mrs.

Jackson wants to put out three volumes next year, but I think we can do four.

Okay. I better go. Howie and Susie are coming over in a few minutes.

Love,

Elizabeth

P.S. I got Barb's letter too, which was *very* nice. Are you talking to her yet? If you are, please thank her for me. I'll try to write her again soon.

P.P.S. Emma misses you too.

P.P.P.S. I think my May flower time has come, just like you said. I like that thought.

P.P.P.P.S. No word on my father, though.

May 13

Dear Elizabeth,

Of course I'll share my recipes with you. The marshmallow meat loaf was just for fun . . . kind of a goof . . . but it actually tasted pretty good. Luke ate two pieces. (Whoops . . . I forgot . . . Now he's Lucas . . . but this happened in the good old days when I wasn't mad at him and I called him Luke.) I didn't write down the recipes, but I remember them, and as soon as I have a chance, I'll send them to you. They're easy to make and not expensive. (I know. I know. Send them ASAP!!!!!!) One of them is

Rosemary Chicken. (Doesn't that sound like some-one who's afraid and won't do things? . . . But it's not. And it's really good.) I also have a great maca-roni and cheese dish and this thing that I invented called Chicken Bombay. (I don't remember. Do you like curry? You've got to like curry A LOT for this to work.) Remember my mashed potatoes and Reese's Pieces dish? I don't suppose that's one that you would like. (But it's easy . . . and yummy. Maybe you could substitute granola for the Reese's Pieces.)

It's so wonderful that you have friends at Deer Run. (I am still worried about your safety. Maybe they should rename the place Run, Dear! . . . Was it bad to make a joke like that about it? Sometimes I can't help it that stuff like that just pops into my brain . . . but I'm trying to learn where and when to say it out loud . . . and to whom.) Anyway, I am sooooooo glad that you have friends there, ones who are also on your "staff." Susie is really nice . . . and so is Howie. (He's also soooooooo cute. Hmm.)

Elizabeth . . . thanks for not saying much in your letters about the baby. I really appreciate that. I just don't want to deal with it now.

There's a lot of stuff that I want to ask, to say about your father, but I'm trying not to. I figure that if you are being sooooo good about not talking about the baby (did you ever think about the fact that "baby" is a four-letter word?), then I won't push you to discuss your innermost feelings about your father and what he's done. I do wish that you knew where he was.

Guess what. Everyone here really likes my column in the school paper. (Well, almost everyone . . . one of the teachers told me that I am "irreverent." Look it up in the dictionary and tell me if you agree. Tee-hee.) I don't know what Barbara and Lucas think because I haven't shown them the newspaper.

It's great that you're earning some extra money. I wish I could do that . . . especially now that I'm not asking the Charents for anything. But I don't want to baby-sit anymore.

Anyway, write back soon. I really want to know what's happening.

Love,

Tara*Starr

May 20

Dear Tara*Starr,

Okay, you asked for it! You said you wanted to know what's happening, and suddenly a lot is happening again.

Although I would like to be all perky and tell you about the good stuff (which is also exciting) first, I can't deny that the good stuff is not really the most dramatic or important stuff. So I'll save the cheerful things for later and start off by telling you about . . . my father.

Can you believe it? He finally called. It was so

weird. He called on the very day — the *very* day —
that I had stopped automatically wondering every
time the phone rang if the caller might be Dad. So
when the phone rang at about 8:00 tonight (Sunday)
I was completely unprepared to hear my father's
voice. In fact, I was expecting to hear Susie's, because
I had just called her and she was on the other line
and had said she would call me right back.

Of course, I recognized Dad's voice right away. He
said, "Elizabeth? Hi, it's me, Dad." And I just said, "I
know." I'm sure he was waiting for a big gushy conversation, but the second I heard his voice I felt like
my brain had turned to steel. So instead of saying,
"Where *are* you? I've *missed* you! When are you coming home? Are you okay?" I just said stiffly, "Hold on,
I'll get my mother." (I'm mad at him, Tara. Really
mad at him. It may not seem that way, but I am. How
could I *not* be mad at him?)

I set the phone down on the kitchen table and
ran to get Mom. Since she and Emma were both
tired, they were plunked down in the living room,
watching *The Little Mermaid* together. "Mom," I whis-
pered loudly, "come here." Emma didn't take her

eyes off the screen (or her thumb out of her mouth) when Mom left the room.

When we were in the kitchen I said, "Mom, *Dad* is on the phone." And then, Tara, I did something — well, two things — I know you would be proud of. First I eavesdropped on Mom's end of the conversation from outside the kitchen door, and then I actually picked up the extension in the hallway and listened to the rest of the conversation.

You know that saying about eavesdroppers never hearing anything good? Well, I guess it's true. My father is going to leave us. He wants to get a separation from Mom. I'm not sure where he's been all this time (I missed that part of the conversation, and I haven't pressed Mom for details because she's pretty upset), but he's coming by on Saturday to pick up his stuff. At least he wants to see us before he goes. Where is he going? He didn't really say, but I got the feeling he was leaving town. When I see him on Saturday I am going to *make* him tell us where he's going. Give us an address and a phone number. I have a LOT of questions for him too. I'm going to list them on a sheet of paper, sit across from him in the living room, ask every single one, and make him answer every single one before he leaves.

So that's the news about my father.

Other news is that *Silhouette* is coming along really well. We put up signs about it all over school, and kids have already started sending us poems. I hadn't expected so many, but I guess Mrs. Jackson had. She told us the hardest part of putting together the journal will be deciding which poems are *not* going to be in it. I'm not going to think about that right now. There's an awful lot of other stuff to do anyway. For starters, we need to find a couple of people to do some artwork for the journal. Plus, I'm writing a few poems myself.

School is a lot more fun now that I'm hanging out with Howie and Susie. We eat lunch together most days. And then there are the journal meetings. I feel like I've been asleep since last fall and I'm just waking up.

Emma has a friend here at DEER RUN. He's Susie's brother Matt. They played together last Sunday and invented a game in which they were cars at a gas station. It went on forever and I didn't see any point to it, but they had a lot of fun.

Tara, you mentioned the baby in your last letter. Is it okay for me to bring up the subject now? I won't if you don't want me to. Just let me know.

Well, the next time I write I'll tell you about the visit with my father. I want some answers, and he better give them to me.

Love,

Elizabeth

P.S. Here's an interesting thing concerning my father. He's leaving, but I don't feel sad or even like I'll miss him that much. Mostly I feel angry. I feel like he left us a long, long time ago.

May 24

Dear Elizabeth,

I don't believe your father!!!!!!!!!!!!!!!!!!!!!!!!!!!!!!!!!!!!!
If he weren't your father, I would say terrible, vile
things about him. Instead, I'll just say that I hope he
gets all that he deserves in the world.

You are being soooooooooooooo strong. (And I
am proud of you for eavesdropping and for picking
up the phone and listening in. It may not have been
right in some ways, but I think it was right because
of what's going on.)

It's wonderful that you are talking about how

210

mad you are at your father. Your "brain turning to steel" when you talked to him was pretty amazing. I think that my guts and heart would have turned to fire and then exploded, but I'm really beginning to see that there are different ways to deal with stuff.

What are you going to say? What are you going to ask? If you want to show me, I'd really love to see your list.

As for *Silhouette* . . . I can't wait to see it! I wish I could be part of it. . . . Oh well. . . . I'm writing for the paper here . . . but it isn't the same as writing with kids that I know so well and being on your "staff." (Do you think we'd always get along if I were a member of your "staff"? (Just something I was thinking about.)

Okay . . . You've told me sooooo much. I guess I should tell you what's going on. About the b-word . . . for a long time there wasn't much going on. I wasn't talking to Barb and Luke and they weren't talking to me. Well, actually, I did talk "at" them, and to myself in front of them. Finally, one day, I said to myself, "Oh, look . . . here are the breeders. I wonder if they're going to make the

DemonSeed take care of them too." Well, Elizabeth . . . they stopped trying to win the "Understanding Parents of the Year" award. Boy, did they yell at me! Luke said I was upsetting them at a time when they were very happy about the new baby-to-be. I said, "You mean the Demon Seed." Barb said I am never to use that term again, that I was being an immature, self-involved, selfish child. I said, "It takes one to know one." And then I started to cry, not just cry . . . but sob. I cried for a very long time. At one point, Barb moved close to me as if she were going to hug me, but then she moved back and waited. I just kept crying and then Luke said, "Tell us what you're feeling." So I told them. I told them that I was worried . . . that just when they were FINALLY working steadily and we were beginning to save money and I didn't have to worry all the time, Barb would have the baby . . . and we wouldn't have the money to pay for the hospital and for the baby . . . and that I didn't want to be the sitter all the time . . . that I was tired of taking care of people. . . . Elizabeth, I know this probably sounds selfish, but remember, my mom and dad are only seventeen years older than I am . . . and they were not always so "mature." For a long time, Luke didn't keep a job. Neither of them made much money. Remember how I used to make dinner for them and keep the house organized, how sometimes there was almost no money in the house and none in the bank? I wanted to know if that was going to happen *again*.

Luke and Barb explained a lot of stuff to me. And they apologized for some of the rough times. (I also told them that a lot of the time it wasn't so bad and that they were a lot of fun and not like any other parents I know, and I'm not sure I want to share them.) Anyway, Luke got a promotion during the time I wasn't speaking to them. (They knew it was coming.) That means more money, medical insurance, and the chance for more promotions. Barb is expecting a raise soon . . . and her boss said that she'll get maternity leave and there's a day care center where she works. She expects to work for as long as possible until the baby is born and then go back soon after the D.S. (okay . . . the Baby) is born. And they said that I'm not going to have to baby-sit all the time . . . but that we are a family and we all have to help each other out. They also said that I had to stop acting like such a brat. (I know I was acting like one, but I was really upset!!!!) After they explained things to me I felt better . . . but don't expect me to get all gooey about this baby until I find out what kind of person he or she is. Elizabeth, do you think they make rubber diaper pants with rhinestones and beads and sequins? Anyway . . . phew . . . that was a very long paragraph. We're all talking again . . . and I do love my parents. (They've been promoted again from Charents.) And they love me. (Although we don't always like each other.)

Well, that's about it.

Please write to me IMMEDIATELY after seeing your father.

Love,

Tara Starr

P.S. Shorter Letter Later (*grin*)

Elizabeth

May 26

Dear Tara*Starr,

It is Saturday and I have not seen my father. I'm not going to see him either. I will not get to ask him my list of questions. The questions were all prepared too, sort of like an assignment for school. I wrote them on Monday, then all week I kept looking them over and making changes. On Friday, during study hall, I decided the list was just right and I copied it over neatly. I can still send it to you if you want, but it seems kind of pointless since I didn't get to *ask* the questions.

Why am I not going to see my father? Because he chickened out, that's why. He's a big, stupid, drunk baby and I hate him. He's spoiled too. Because he got all his stuff, just like he wanted, only he did it without seeing Mom and Emma and me.

This is what happened. After school yesterday, Howie and Susie and I walked home as usual. We had just walked between those brick walls that say DEER on one side and RUN on the other, when Mrs. Haslin called to me from her office. (She's one of the managers of DEER RUN.)

She said, "Elizabeth! Hi, I'm glad I caught you. Here are your keys." And I said, "What keys?" and she said, "Your father's. He thought you'd like them as a spare set." I must have looked awfully confused, because Mrs. Haslin said, "He dropped them off here after he picked up his things."

I knew that Mrs. Haslin knew that Mom and Dad had split up (Mom had told her a couple of days ago), but I couldn't figure out why Mrs. Haslin thought Dad had already picked up his stuff. Then a terrible thought occurred to me and I got this hollow feeling in my stomach. I took the keys from Mrs. Haslin, told Susie and Howie I would see them later, and ran all the way to our apartment. I opened the door and burst into the living room. Sure enough, all Dad's things were gone.

My father came early, Tara. He came when he knew we wouldn't be home, and he took his stuff and left without seeing us. He didn't even leave a note.

I was going to write more. I was going to ask you some things about Barb and Luke and the baby, and tell you about *Silhouette*, but you know what? I just can't right now. I'll have to write again, okay? When I'm feeling better. I *am* really happy that you and your parents are talking, though. And that everything seems to be under control with the baby.

Love,

Elizabeth

P.S. This time it's my turn to say **L**onger **L**etter **L**ater

P.P.S. Did I say that I hate my father? (Mom says she guesses he isn't ever coming back.)

May 30

Dear Elizabeth,

You know how rare it is for me to say, "I don't know what to say." But I don't know what to say.

Is there anything I can do to help?

Should we call so that you can talk to us? (I know how much you like to tell things to Barb.)

There are lots of things I want to say about your father, lots of names I want to call him . . . but something tells me that's not a good idea. I'm glad, though, that you are saying things about him. I never thought you would talk like that.

218

How is your mom doing? Emma? How are you doing?

I keep wishing there was some way to work things out.

I don't think it's fair for some grown-ups to make things so awful for some kids.

I don't think it's fair that it's happening to you and Emma.

It shouldn't happen to anyone.

I'm thinking about you lots . . . and worrying about you lots.

Write back as soon as you can.

Love,

Tara Starr

June 7

Dear Tara*Starr,

I'm sorry for not writing back sooner. I just wanted to let a little time go by so I could calm down. Also, I have to admit that I was kind of waiting to see if my father would get in touch with us. I know that's silly, but I just thought he *might*. And then I would have been able to tell you that I yelled at him or something. But of course he hasn't been in touch. So the news on that front is that we're just dealing. Emma is probably dealing the best because she never even knew he was supposed to come by the apartment. Mom very wisely had said not to tell her because she thought Emma would get overly excited, and she'd have a heart attack trying to wait five days to see him. Also, I think Mom thought there was a chance that Dad wouldn't show up, and she didn't want Emma to be disappointed. (Mom was smarter than I was.) So anyway, Emma is okay. I think she kind of forgets about Dad for long periods of time, which is good. But it's hard to know how to answer her when she asks if she'll ever see Daddy again.

Mom and I are okay too. Not great, just okay. Thank you for the offer to talk to Barb, but you know what? I love talking to Barb, but Mom and I have been talking a lot lately. More than ever. My mother probably says different things to me than Barb would say. I don't mind. Different is just different. And Mom and I are being very honest with each other. I told her that sometimes I wish Dad would die, and she said it was okay to feel that way, and that she understood.

I don't know why Dad did what he did this year. I don't think it's because he hates us. I don't think it's because he's a bad person. But I suppose something went wrong and he felt like he was falling apart.

Maybe he did fall apart. Like when you used to hear that someone had a "nervous breakdown." Drinking made things worse, losing his job made things worse. And then he lost his lifestyle. Why were Mom and I able to cope when Dad couldn't? I don't know. Why does anything happen? Why does someone in a family get cancer when everyone else is healthy? Something went wrong in my father. This is what I've decided recently: I hate what my father did to us, but I don't hate him. I can't. Just like I couldn't hate someone for getting cancer.

I think there are a lot of things I'll never know about my father.

I have exciting news about *Silhouette*. Our first issue is going to come out in nine days, one week before the last day of school. I am so happy about it! Lots of kids submitted really great poems (Mrs. Jackson helped us write notes to the kids whose poems we didn't use), and we found a great artist. Shawnelle Wagner. Do you remember her? (She's in eighth grade, so unfortunately she won't be able to illustrate the *Silhouette* next year.) One night last week Howie and Susie came over and we worked until 11:38 P.M.

on *Silhouette*. There was so much to do, but it was all fun.

Guess what we decided to do this summer. Howie and Susie and I, I mean. We're going to start our own poetry workshop and get together every Tuesday and Thursday night to read and discuss poetry (the library has a *great* poetry section). Also, we are going to try to have ice-cream night every Saturday. Also, we are going to try to spend as much time together as possible! We all have jobs, though. I am going to be full-time in charge of Emma this summer. Mom says I'm cheaper than the day care center. Howie is going to do something with computers. He set up his own business. He'll be helping people who are having trouble with their computers. Susie is working for her mother, helping her with the desktop publishing. She was going to go into business with Howie, since she knows even more about computers than he does, but her mother kind of needs her. Susie doesn't mind. She likes the desktop publishing stuff, too.

I'm looking forward to the summer, Tara. I need to relax. Did I tell you there are pools at DEER RUN — a regular pool and a baby pool. I can take

Emma swimming every day. I got a new bathing suit and I like the way I look in it.

I'll send you a copy of *Silhouette* when it comes out!!!

Lots of love,

Elizabeth

June 10

Dear Elizabeth,

You sound so much better. You actually sound happy!!!!! (Well, except for the stuff about your father, and it sounds like you've thought about how you can deal with it.)

I'm so glad that *Silhouette* is going well and that you're friends with Howie and Susie.

I'm going to catch you up on a lot of stuff (in a list . . . it's easier for me that way . . . you know how my mind . . . and mouth . . . sometimes go so fast that it gets confusing).

1. My looks ... I've gotten sooooo much taller this year. My normally brownish-blond hair has a purple streak in it. (A couple of my friends and I just got bored one day and we all streaked our hair. ... . Hannah has a magenta streak, Allie a green one, and John a silver one.) Barb and Luke are not crazy about it. We have had "a little discussion," and I've promised not to do anything extreme to my body without getting permission first. They were afraid that I was going to do something like get my tongue pierced, but I wouldn't be that dumb. One of the guys in eighth grade did that. Can you imagine what it would be like to kiss him????? (Yeech!!! Much worse than a Chee-to kiss, I bet.)

2. I have been writing lots too ... but not poetry. I've been writing funny things for the school paper. The kids here really like what I've done. Some of the teachers (and cafeteria cooks) are not so happy. The principal and I had a little talk about free speech vs. other people's feelings. ... . But I think that a menu

that always tastes like hot-dog water, no matter what is being served, deserves to be written about . . . and teachers who sneak out of school during their breaks, sit in their cars, and have a cigarette deserve to be busted.

3. My grades. . . . You know how I always used to get lectures about "not working up to my potential." Well, Elizabeth . . . I have been. Last marking period I got all A's, except for a C in math (where I was working up to my potential. I'm just a potentially pathetic person when it comes to math). In fact, I've been recommended to be part of a tutoring program next year. (Great, huh?!!!!)

4. My friends . . . Elizabeth, they are so much fun. We can all be funny together . . . and when there's serious stuff going on, we can all talk about it. I know lots of different people . . . the kids in the drama group, the ones on the school newspaper, the Chess Club (I know . . . I don't play chess . . . but they're nice kids). I'm thinking of joining the fencing team. The kids here are really great.

(Well, not all of them . . . that's another story . . . but most of them.)

Elizabeth — I have a great idea. Come visit me for a week this summer. That way you can see everything in person. I know that you have to baby-sit for Emma, but maybe you and your mom can work something out. (It sounds like you could really use a vacation.) I know that you're going to be busy with work and your writing group, but I miss you soooo much and I really want us to see each other.

So much has happened this school year. Sometimes I think that we're both so different that we aren't going to be friends someday, that we'll just go our own ways. I DON'T WANT THAT TO HAPPEN. I really want for us to be friends forever, so I think we have to see each other face-to-face, to be able to talk about things without having to wait for letters.

Anyway, Barb and Luke say that if you can find a way to get here, they'll pay all of your expenses while you're here (food, going places, etc.). They miss you too.

Please . . . oh, please . . . oh, please. Come visit.

This will be the last time that we'll have a chance to be alone before the D.S. arrives. (Don't worry. When I say D.S., I'm not calling it the Demon Seed anymore. It's now the Dear Sibling. Hah.)

Oh, Elizabeth . . . it would be so great if you could visit. When you write, I know the kids you are talking about and where you live (although I've never been to your new place). I want you to know where I am.

We'll have a great time . . . and guess what . . . I have a new boyfriend. His name is Bart. (He's really intelligent. I call him Bart the Smart.) He's got a best friend, Jeff, who isn't going out with anyone, so when you get here we can double-date.

And Elizabeth . . . just think . . . We can show each other our writing in person (not just our letter writing). Then, when we become famous authors, we can tell people how we've always helped each other out.

Please, oh please, try to visit.

Love,

Tara Starr

June 17

Dear Tara*Starr,

Yes, yes, yes, I would love to come for a visit! And guess what — I can!! I already worked everything out. Here's how:

1. Airline ticket — Mom has frequent-flyer miles left over from last year, and she says there are definitely enough for a round-trip flight to Ohio.

2. Spending money — I have saved a lot of baby-sitting money. I used some of it to buy my bathing suit and a few other things I needed, but I have most of it, and I'll have even more, depending on how long I've been taking care of Emma before I leave for Ohio. By the way, THANK YOU THANK YOU THANK YOU to Barb and Luke and you for offering to pay for all of my other expenses. That is so sweet, but I might be able to pay for *most* of them with my own money.

3. Emma — While I'm visiting you, Susie is going to take over my job. She says her mother will be able to spare her, plus my mom pays better than her mom, *plus* she adores Emma, and Emma and Matt can play together.

4. Timing — Mom says I can visit whenever it's a good time for you and Barb and Luke. I just have to let Susie know ahead of time so she can make her plans.

Also, Mom adds THANK YOU THANK YOU THANK YOU to Barb and Luke and you for asking me to visit and offering to pay for stuff (and probably for a lot of other things too).

Tara, I'm looking forward to meeting Hannah and Bart and everyone in person. A double-date sounds like fun.

So when can I come? Please let me know. I am so excited I can't stand it!!!

Love,

Elizabeth

P.S. I want to be friends forever too.

P.P.S. A *purple* streak? In your *hair*???!

June 22

Dear Elizabeth,

ZOUNDS!!!!!!!GADZOOKS!!!!!!!!! HOORAY.

I am soooooooooooooo happy.

I can't believe it.

You can actually visit!!!!!!!!!!!!!!!!!!!!!!!!!!!!!!!!!!

Hug your mom for me and say THANK YOU THANK YOU THANK YOU THANK YOU THANK YOU. (And give Emma a hug just because I miss her.)

You can come here anytime, whatever's best for you and your family. What's best for me is that you get here ASAP (that's not only "as soon as